P9-BYC-086

RANDOM
HOUSE
LARGE
PRINT

THE WEEKEND

RANDOM HOUSE
LARGE PRINT

THE WEEKEND

CHARLOTTE WOOD

First published in paperback in Australia by Allen & Unwin, Sydney, 2019
First American edition published by Riverhead Books, 2020

Published in the United States of America by Random House Large Print in association with Riverhead Books, an imprint of Penguin Random House LLC.

Cover design by Lauren Peters-Collaer
Cover illustration by Jessica Brilli

The Library of Congress has established a Cataloging-in-Publication record for this title.

ISBN: 978-0-593-28601-2

www.penguinrandomhouse.com/large-print-format-books

FIRST LARGE PRINT EDITION

Printed in the United States of America

10 9 8 7 6 5 4 3 2 1

This Large Print edition published in accord with the standards of the N.A.V.H.

For Sean,
and for my friends

Dreams & beasts are two keys by which we are to find out the secrets of our own nature.

RALPH WALDO EMERSON

THE WEEKEND

CHAPTER ONE

It was not the first time it had happened, this waking early in the pale light with a quiet but urgent desire to go to church.

Cognitive decline, doubtless. Frontal-lobe damage, religion, fear of death—they were all the same thing. Jude had no illusions.

This longing—was it a longing? It was mysterious, an insistence inside her, a sort of ache that came and went, familiar and yet still powerful and surprising when it arrived. Like the arthritis that flared at the base of her thumb. The point was, this feeling had nothing to do with Christmas or with anything in her waking life. It came somehow from the world of sleep, from her dreaming self.

At first when it came, it would trouble her, but now Jude gave herself over to it. She lay in her white bed on the morning before Christmas Eve and imagined the cool, dark space of a cathedral, where she might be alone, welcomed by some unseen, velvety force. She imagined herself kneeling, resting her head on the ancient wood of the pew in front of her, and closing her eyes. It was peaceful, in that quiet space of her imagination.

Frontal-lobe shrinkage, doubtless. At this age it was inevitable.

She pictured the soft gray sphere of her brain and remembered lambs' brains on a plate. She used to enjoy eating brains; it was one of the dishes she ordered often with Daniel. But the last time she did—three tender, tiny things lined up along a rectangular plate—she was revolted. Each one was so small you could fit it in a dessert spoon, and in this fashionable Turkish restaurant they were unadorned, undisguised by crumbs or garnish, just three bald, poached splotches on a bed of green. She ate them, of course she did, it was part of her code: You did not refuse what was offered. Chosen, indeed, here. But at first bite, the thing yielded in her mouth, too rich, like just-soft butter, tepid and pale gray, the color and taste of moths or death. In that moment she was shocked into a vision of the three lambs, each one its own conscious self, with its own senses, its intimate pleasures and pains. After a mouthful she could not go on, and Daniel ate the rest. She had wanted to say, **I don't want to die.**

Of course she did not say that. Instead she asked Daniel about the novel he was reading. William Maxwell, or William Trevor, she often confused the two. He was a good reader, Daniel. A true reader.

Daniel laughed at men who did not read fiction, which was nearly all the men he knew. They were afraid of something in themselves, he said. Afraid of being shown up, of not understanding—or more likely the opposite: They would be led **to** understanding themselves, and it scared the shit out of them. Daniel snorted. They said they didn't have time for it, which was the biggest joke of all.

Jude pulled the sheet up to her chin. The day felt sticky already; the sheet was cool over her clammy body.

What would happen if she did not wake, one of these mornings? If she died one night in her bed? Nobody would know. Days would pass. Eventually Daniel would call and get no answer. Then what? They had never discussed this: what to do if she died in her bed.

Last Christmas, Sylvie was here, and this one she wasn't—and now they were going to clear out the house at Bittoes. **Take anything you want,** Gail had said to them from Dublin in an e-mail. **Have**

a holiday. How you could think cleaning your dead friend's house a holiday . . . but it was Christmas, and Gail felt guilty for flitting off back to Ireland and leaving it to them. So. Take anything you want.

There was nothing Jude wanted. She couldn't speak for the others.

Sylvie had been in the ground for eleven months.

The memorial had been in the restaurant (unrecognizable now from the old days—everything but the name had gone), and there were beautiful food and good champagne, good speeches. Wendy spoke brilliantly, honestly, poetically. Gail lurched with a silent, terrible sobbing, with Sylvie's poor sad brother, Colin, beside her, unable to touch Gail for comfort. He was eighty-one; he'd been a greenskeeper at the golf club in their hometown, stayed long after the rest of the family left. Never managed to get over his sister's being gay.

In the end Sylvie went where nobody expected: an old-fashioned burial in Mona Vale, next to her parents. To this part Jude and Wendy and Adele went with Colin, and Gail, and Andy and Elektra from the old days. There they'd all stood in the hot cemetery with a sympathetic priest (a priest! for Sylvie!), and Jude had picked up a handful of dirt and thrown it down. Strange that in all these years it was the first time she'd ever done that, or even seen it done outside a film. She felt silly squatting in the dirt, scrabbling in the dry gravel with her polished nails, but when she stretched and flung and let the earth rain down on Sylvie's coffin, a breath of awful sorrow swept through her, up and out of her body into the deafening, glittering white noise of the cicadas.

Sylvie was dead and felt no pain. They had said good-bye. Nothing was left to regret, but she was still in there, in that box, under the weight of all that earth, her cold little body rotted away.

Gail said she looked peaceful at the end. But that wasn't peace; it was absence of muscle tone, of life. Being dead made you look younger, it was a fact. Jude had seen six or seven dead faces now, and they all, in the moment after life left, smoothed out and looked like their much younger selves. Even like babies once or twice.

How long did it take a corpse to rot? Sylvie would screech at a question like that. **You're so** ghoulish, **Jude.**

The ceiling fan in her bedroom rotated slowly, ticking, above her. Her life was as clean and bare as a bone, bare as that white blade, its path through the unresisting air absolutely known, unwavering. This should be a comfort. It **was** a comfort. The rooms of her apartment were uncluttered by the past. Nobody would have to plow through dusty boxes and cupboards full of rubbish for Jude.

She lay in her bed and thought of cathedrals. And she thought of animals: rats beneath the floorboards, cockroaches bristling behind the crossed ankles and bleeding feet of plaster Jesuses. She thought of dark, malevolent little birds; of the muffled small sounds of creatures dying in the spaces between bricks and plaster, between ceilings and roof beams. She thought of their shit drying out and turning hard, and what happened to their skin and fur and organs, rotting unconsecrated in roof cavities.

She would not go to church, obviously, for she was neither a fool nor a coward.

She would go instead to the butcher and the grocer and then the hardware store for the few remaining cleaning things, and she would drive without hurrying along the freeway to the coast, and this afternoon the others would arrive.

It was not a holiday, the three women had warned one another, but the warning was really for Adele, who would disappear at the first sign of work. Adele would be useless, but they couldn't leave her out.

It was only three days. Two, really, given that most of today would be filled with the shopping and driving and arriving. And on Boxing Day the other two would leave and Daniel would come. She watched the fan blade's smooth glide. She would be like this: unhurried, gliding calmly through the hours until Adele and Wendy left. She would not let the usual things get to her; they were all too old for that.

It occurred to her that one of them could be next to go. Funny how she'd not thought of that until this moment. She threw off the sheet in a clean white billow.

After her shower, though, while she was making the bed, already some little flecks of annoyance with Wendy began creeping in. It was like dipping a hand into a pocket and searching the seams with your fingers; there would always be some tiny irritant crumbs if she wanted to find them. Why, for example, had Wendy refused a lift, insisting on making the trip in that terrible shitbox of hers? Jude snapped the sheet, fending off the affront that would come if she let it, about Wendy's secretive refusal to explain. Jude's hospitality, not just in the long-gone restaurant days but in general terms, was well known. People said it about her, had always done so. She guarded her generosity even more as they all grew older and she saw other women become irrationally fearful about money and turn miserly. Pinching coins out of their purses in cafés, bargaining in charity shops. Holding out their hands for twenty cents' change. It was appalling. It was beneath them.

Yet now, as she folded hospital corners—her bulging disk threatened to twang, but she maneuvered carefully and eased around it—she considered the possibility that hidden within the compliments about her largesse might be needles of sarcasm. Once her sister-in-law had murmured, "It's not that generous if you have to keep mentioning it," and Jude had burned with silent rage. Burned and burned.

If she told Daniel about any of this, if she complained about Wendy and the car, he'd shake his head and tell her she had too much time on her hands.

She yanked another corner of the sheet.

If Sylvie were here, Jude could phone her and find out what the matter was with

Wendy, and they could be exasperated together and then agree that it didn't matter, and Jude would be able to compose herself for when Wendy parked her filthy, battered car in the driveway at Bittoes, and she would be calm and welcoming and free of grievance. Now she would have to do it by herself.

This was something nobody talked about: How death could make you petty. And how you had to find a new arrangement among your friends, shuffling around the gap of the lost one, all of you suddenly mystified by how to be with one another.

With other circles of friends, a death meant you were permitted to quietly go your separate ways. After the first shocks, the early ones in your forties and fifties—the accidents and suicides and freak diseases, the ones that orphaned children, shook the ground beneath cities—when you reached your seventies and the disintegration began in earnest, there was the understanding, never spoken, that the latest—the news of another stroke, a surprise death, a tumor or an Alzheimer's diagnosis—would not be the last. A certain amount of withdrawal was acceptable. Within reason you did what you must, to protect yourself. From what? Jude stood, looking down at the flat, white space of the bed. From all that . . . emotion. She turned and left the room.

It was true that time had gradually taken on a different cast. It didn't seem to go forward or backward now, but up and down. The past was striated through you, through your body, leaching into the present and the future. The striations were evident, these streaky layers of memory, of experience—but you were one being, you contained all of it. If you looked behind or ahead of you, all was emptiness.

When she'd told Daniel—crying bitterly, smoking—what Sylvie had said in the hospital about Wendy and Adele, he gazed at her with soft reproach and said, "But, Judo, of course you will, because you **do** love them. Because they're your dearest friends."

Daniel was quite sentimental, really.

It could be oddly appealing in a man. Why was that, when in a woman it was so detestable?

She sat at the dining table to drink her coffee. It was 7:34. If she got to the grocer by 8:15, she might find a parking space quickly, and then she could be in and out of the butcher and then the hardware place, home, and packed, and on the road by 9:30. Ten latest. She reached for the notepad with the list, swished it toward herself.

People went on about how death brought people together, but it wasn't true. The graveyard, the stony dirt—that's what it was like now. The topsoil had blown away and left only bedrock. It was embarrassing, somehow, to pretend they could return to the softness that had once cushioned their dealings with one another. Despite the fact that the three women knew one another better than they did their own siblings, Sylvie's death had opened up strange caverns of distance between them.

She wrote: **scourers.**

And it had opened up great oceans of

anger in Jude, which shocked her. Now when other people died, she found the mention of it offensive. It was Sylvie who had died, who was to be mourned. Other people's neighbors and sisters were of no relevance; why did people keep telling her about them? Even Daniel! Holding her hand in his one evening, telling her his cousin Roger had gone, a heart attack on a boat. Jude had waited for him to come to the point before realizing it was sympathy he wanted. From her. It was all she could do not to spit on the floor. She had to put a hand to her mouth, the force of her need to spit was so great. She wanted to shout, **So what, Andrew died—of course he did!** What did Daniel expect? Everybody **died.** But not Sylvie.

She looked at the list again. Adele had been at her about the pavlova. She knew it wasn't a holiday, but it's **Christmas,** Jude, it's a **tradition.** Adele had always been soppy about things like this. Though actors were sentimental, in Jude's experience;

she supposed they had to be. They had to be able to believe in all sorts of things.

But the humidity would make a meringue collapse; it was going to be so wretchedly hot. They were all too fat anyway, especially Wendy. Christmas be damned, they could have fruit and yogurt. She put a line through **eggs.**

She had not spit on the floor, and she had not pulled her hand away from Daniel's, and she said she was sorry even though all she felt for his dead cousin was shame, that he might try to associate himself with what had happened to Sylvie.

She stopped, looked at her list. **Don't be so hard on people, Jude.** She added **eggs** again.

Jude hated having other candles lit next to the one she secretly thought of as Sylvie's, in the cathedral she had stolen into once or twice. Sometimes she blew the other candles out.

None of this could be said. She lied in all the expected ways.

• • • •

Wendy ran her hand down the length of Finn's sweaty, narrow back. "It's all right, boyo, it's all right."

In her dented red Honda by the side of the freeway under the hot blue sky, she crooned softly to the dog who had clambered into the front and was trying to claw his way onto her lap. She hardly had room even to lean sideways but managed to release the lever: her seat slid all the way back with a chunking sound, and Finn landed heavily across her body. It was so hot here in the airless car.

She sat with her head pressed back against the seat, listening to the rhythmic on-off click of the hazard lights and the dog's anxious whining, and looked out the window. She could see only the looming rush of car-ghosts into and then past her side-view mirror, and the grays and greens of scrub and road. For a moment she spiraled out and away from herself and Finn and the car into a high, aerial view of the bush and the road. She saw her car, a tiny red blob huddled beneath the great stone cliff on the freeway between the city and the coast. And then she plummeted down again and felt the panic of the landing, here in her present circumstances.

Finn whined and licked his lips and did not settle but instead tried to turn his large, shaggy body around in the small space, treading again over Wendy's thighs, shifting his weight, his claws catching in the thin fabric of her trousers. He couldn't pace his circles in the car; he would get more and more agitated. She'd hoped he would sleep all the way, but now the car had broken down and he was frightened, and Bittoes was still an hour away, and it was so muggy she could hardly breathe.

There was nothing to do but wait. She had found the roadside assistance number and called, and although her membership had lapsed, she could just pay the extra—**thank God, thank God** for mobile phones, thank God for credit cards. Sometimes the modern world was filled with miraculous goodness. Her phone battery had been full. Or half full. She extracted this merciful fact from the guilty chaos inside herself. She wasn't so hopeless as to have a flat phone battery as well.

But the adrenaline of moments ago was still spreading through her body, the echo of it hot and cold and chemical like gin or anesthetic along her veins and through the core of her bones. She'd forgotten how it felt until the moment it happened. The soaking dread of a vehicle stuttering beneath you, suddenly dropping all power as you ascended a hill at a hundred and fifteen kilometers an hour with a line of cars barreling along behind you. She'd forgotten the drench of disbelief as the car faltered, forgotten the sound of your own voice calling out, **No no please please come on, little car, just hang on,** as you pumped and pumped the accelerator, lurching to the side of the road, and the cars behind you were forced to brake suddenly, then roar past in perilous, swerving overtaking, horns blaring, drivers screaming abuse, and all the time Wendy calling out, "It's all right, Finny, it's all right," to the ancient dog curled on his smelly tartan bed on the backseat.

But he had already lifted his grubby head and begun whining, staring anxiously about while Wendy's heart hammered in her chest and she pulled over into the breakdown lane, drawing as close as she could to the great stone wall of the dark cliff face.

And now they just had to wait. There was nothing to panic about now. Except to please, please not have Finn piss in the car.

It was so **sticky.** And despite the clear skies, storms were forecast in the coming days. Wendy pushed this to the bottom of her mind, into that marsh of things not to be thought about. Finn whined again now. She would need to get him out of the car for the toilet if the roadside assistance did not turn up soon. But the girl on the phone had said it would be at least an hour and a half. When Wendy exclaimed at this, the girl said—patiently, as if Wendy were an imbecile—"We're leading in to Christmas, you see. Everyone's on the road."

The car shuddered again as another trailer truck whumped past. It had been thirty degrees when they left home, probably hotter now. It was intolerably stuffy without the air-conditioning. The humidity pressed in through the cracks in the car's chassis, coating Wendy and Finn. Sweaty, oppressive.

He would need to wee, but how could she possibly get him out? The driver's side was impossible, the holiday traffic roaring past; she had a fleeting vision of their two frail bodies obliterated by a truck. Bits of arm and hindquarter raining down. But on the passenger side was the sheer rock wall, too close for her to squeeze out of the door, and she could not let him out alone.

She put the radio on. A melodic drift of guitar, the Pretenders singing about Christmastime. She rocked softly, and Finn was slumped in her lap now, heavy, unbearably hot, but quiet. So she sat.

Once she had known how to open a car

hood and whack the alternator with a tire iron to get it going again. Once she had driven all the way from Lithgow to Dubbo doing this, in the dark, getting out, opening the hood and whacking the part every forty-five kilometers. She'd felt absolutely no fear. That was the days before mobile phones. Women were braver then.

Technology and female fear, that was interesting. That could go in with the stuff she had already done on dependence. Or in an earlier chapter. Somewhere. If she could get out of the car now, she would like to see what the tire iron felt like in her hand again. The weight of such a thing, she hadn't felt that in years. People used them for violence—there could be something in that, too.

"Come on, Finny, move over."

She lifted his great forepaws and shoved at him, trying to move him to the passenger side at least. Her leg was going to sleep under his weight, and she needed more air. But he wriggled backward, farther into her lap, and braced his arthritic front paws even harder against her knees, his claws digging and scratching. His whining began again, higher and more frightened.

When was the time she'd had to whack the alternator? She counted back—using her books, the ages of her children, Lance's jobs—to discover she must have been thirty-two, thirty-three. It was the Subaru, with the kids' bikes in the back. But Claire was fifty-four now. So it was a very long time ago. Did cars even have alternators anymore? Wendy could not get out, so she would never know.

Finn's fetid breath rose up. When he was a puppy she could hold him along one arm, wearing him, a woolly white gauntlet. Now he was enormous, a hot, immovable weight in her lap. It was hopeless. She turned her face from the smell of him and wound down the window a little. She patted him comfortingly with firm, rhythmic thuds of her hand.

Mobile phones gave you a sense of permanent rescuability. A false sense, obviously. She would write that into the chapter. She could not call Claire, because Claire had been at her for years to get a new car. And what would she do about it anyway? Wendy was confused by many things about Claire, but her ice-cold perfect manners were the most shocking. Where did a person learn that smooth, corporate-management way of speaking to her own mother? Whenever Wendy spoke to Claire on the phone, it was like ringing a complaint hotline; the assertiveness training did all the work. **Unfortunately, I'm unable to offer . . . What I propose is . . .** If Wendy had to write down an emergency contact on a form, she put Claire, but sitting here now she thought how mistaken this was, because Claire might not actually come if her mother were, say, found in bloody, fleshy shreds on a road. She would make some calls and go back to work. She would send flowers to the funeral. Whatever happened to daughter's guilt? The world had changed. Or what about simple familial duty . . . ?

But this was bad, this was her own

mother's way of thinking. Self-indulgent and mean. Wendy detested conservatism. Everybody hated old people now; it was acceptable, encouraged even, because of your paid-off mortgage and your free education and your ruination of the planet. And Wendy agreed. She loathed nostalgia, the past bored her. More than anything she despised self-pity. And they **had** been lucky. And wasteful. They had failed to protect the future. But, on the other hand, she and Lance had had nothing when they were young. Nothing! The Claires of the world seemed to forget that, with all their trips to Europe, their coffee machines and air conditioners and three bathrooms in every house. And anyway, lots of people, lots of **women**—Wendy felt a satisfying feminist righteousness rising—didn't have paid-off mortgages, had no retirement savings. Look at Adele, living on air.

Thank the Lord God that Adele had gotten herself set up with Liz, was what Wendy thought about that.

So it was true Wendy had nothing to complain about. Except here she was, with an elderly, demented dog, broken down on the side of the road in thirty-three degrees.

On the phone to the roadside service, she'd hesitated but added in a quiet, hopeful, dignified way, "I'm seventy-five." Then hated herself for it when the girl didn't skip a beat, just repeated her singsong assurance, first-available-take-care-have-a-merry-Christmas.

It really was hot now.

She could phone Jude, who might not be ahead of her on the road and who could glide into place beside them in her sleek, dark Audi. But there was something of the undertaker about Jude. She radiated a kind of grim satisfaction when things went wrong for other people. Plus, she'd been snippy about Wendy's saying no to a lift. Jude's car was serviced every six months whether she had driven it or not. And despite being garaged, it was washed—professionally—once a fortnight. Once a

fortnight! In this time of catastrophic climate change! Jude's insurance and registration papers would be in a special folder, and she would know where that folder was, and she had probably never used roadside assistance in her life because ever since she got involved with Daniel all her cars were brand new, so no, she could not be asked for help.

Wendy rubbed Finn's head and said, "We couldn't ask her, could we, Finny? Not old Jude."

No wonder Jude had never been a mother. It would offend her sense of order.

Sylvie would have helped. She would shout down the phone in exasperation—**Fucking hell, that bloody car, I told you**—and then she would help. It would be a problem shared, with Sylvie; it would not occur to her that here might be a chance to teach, or reproach. Or humiliate. Wendy missed her more and more.

Also, Wendy had not yet told Jude she was bringing Finn.

She groped down beside the seat for a plastic water bottle—warm, but three-quarters full—and her movement against him as she did so made him squirm and let out an odd moan. How could Wendy still be so afraid of Jude and her silent rebukes? She tried shoving at Finn again, but he would not be moved.

It was exhausting, being friends. Had they ever been able to tell each other the truth?

Then Finn started the trembling.

"Shhhhhh, oh, Finny Fin," Wendy crooned, nuzzling into his bony, hairy back. There was so little flesh on him now.

With difficulty she undid the bottle and took a swig of the warm, plasticky water. It was foul, tainted, but it was important to stay hydrated. Delicately she poured a little of the water into the cap and held it to Finn's mouth. His great soft tongue came out and knocked the cap from her hand to the floor. His tremor worsened. She poured the rest of the water in slops into her hand, and Finn gently lapped and licked at it, and he began to calm down, and the trembling subsided.

Another road train went past; the car swayed violently.

Wendy jumped at the phone suddenly chirping, vibrating under her thigh. Finn lurched again, hurting her legs. He looked at Wendy and whined louder. She struggled to extract the phone, pushing his head away. It was Adele.

When Wendy said hello, a finger pressed into her other ear to block the highway noise, Adele didn't greet her, just demanded, "Where are you?"

"Oh, on the road," Wendy said as cheerfully as possible. "Just pulled over to answer."

"What's that noise?" Adele said.

Wendy tucked the phone into her neck and clamped Finn's snout together, still stroking him, begging him with her eyes to be quiet.

"Nothing!" she shouted, grateful as another huge truck roared past. "I'm not supposed to park here," she said.

Adele was waiting for the train. She sounded odd.

"**Waiting** for it? You said you'd be first to get there, hours ago!" said Wendy. It didn't matter, but Jude would be angry. "What's wrong?"

Adele ignored the question. Just quickly, did Wendy think she could spot her a bit of cash? Only till next week.

Wendy gripped Finn's nose. "How much?"

She felt a little wall of suspicion flip up inside herself. Adele spoke lightly, as if this were an ordinary thing to ask her. She was an actress, after all. You never knew when she was telling the truth. Why wasn't she asking Liz?

Adele answered and Wendy yipped, "Five **hundred**!"

Finn slid his nose from her grip and groaned. At the end of the phone, Adele was triumphant. "Is that Finn! Oh, my God, does Jude know you're bringing him?"

Wendy needed to end this conversation immediately. Yes, she could lend Adele the money, she told her, and now she had to go.

"See you there," Adele said gaily.

Wendy lay back in her seat and closed her eyes, for there was nothing to be done. She shoved the phone beneath her legs and Finn began his treading again, over her thighs, trying to pace his circles. She wished she had never gotten into the car. Why hadn't she just stayed home?

"Come on, Finny boy, come on," she wheedled, and soon he sat again, smelly, heavy in her lap. She kept stroking him, and as she did, she began to count her breaths as the meditation-app man had taught her, and she felt Finn relaxing.

Near the end Sylvie had told her she must remember to look after the others, she must not be neglectful. Wendy had been stung for a moment, not knowing what this meant, but Sylvie was on a lot of morphine then. She'd cried, with Sylvie's creamy hand in hers, and promised.

But what about Gail, going back to Ireland straight after? Almost straight after. The Paddington house cleared out, one go, wiped out like a sick bowl. **Poor Gail,** people said. **Losing the love of your life.** Wendy had to look away each time, had to clean beneath a fingernail with great concentration, to not shout, **But I did! I lost the love of** my **life!**

First Lance, now Sylvie.

Lance died—**a long time ago,** she told herself sternly—and now Sylvie had died, and only Wendy knew that Sylvie was like a goddess. That's what Wendy secretly thought. It was ridiculous, unsayable, but for Wendy, near the end, Sylvie had been like a goddess in a golden robe, ascending, shedding herself, her body, shedding love, shedding fear, shedding illness and sadness. Poor Sylvie had to shed Gail, too, and that was the last, worst thing. She had to work very hard at leaving Gail, like pushing a huge stone from her path. Poor Gail—for watching Sylvie die, Wendy knew, was like watching Lance. Like watching someone being born: the primal instinct, the exhaustion of it, the panting, animal labor.

Watching, wanting it to be over, unable to bear its going on.

Then, when it was finally over, the terrible new avalanche: he was actually gone.

Wendy wanted to say all this at the memorial, but it couldn't be said, obviously. So she talked about their letters from when they met at Oxford and how generous Sylvie was, a fellow Australian, how intelligent and dignified. And then she said plainly she would miss her ("miss" her, anodyne as a greeting card: pathetic, grotesque), and then she stepped away from the microphone. It was decorous, and it was not what she believed, it was not this force that stayed in her all the time now, the column of shimmered gold that was Sylvie, dead.

And Wendy had promised. So she had to come and clean out the beach house, and she had to give Adele the money, and Jude would just have to cope about the damned bloody dog.

She exhaled, long and slow, a restfulness beginning to drift over her, and at that moment she felt the horrible, inevitable flood of the dog's hot piss soaking her lap and her trousers. "Oh, **Finn.**" She held her breath as her poor boy's piss trickled down to soak the cloth of the upholstery beneath her, and the hot misery of it mingled with the salt of her own tears on her skin and the sticky, unbearable heat of this impossible day. She patted poor Finn, wound down the window a little more, and went back to counting her breaths.

She was woken by a hand pushing at her shoulder. She jerked, and Finn yelped in fear. She finally heaved the dog off herself, with a great wrenching that strained something in her shoulder and sent a shooting star of agony into her skull, as the roadside-assistance man yanked open her door.

Mercy! she wanted to cry, and bow down. Instead she shouted, "Hello!" at the same time as the man said, "Jesus Christ, I thought you were dead."

But Wendy was so relieved to see him that she sprang out of the vehicle into the hot, slippery wind, forcing him to flatten himself against the car, and she did not care that he stared down at her sodden pants and thought that she had wet herself.

CHAPTER TWO

Jude parked in the driveway on the flat ground below the house, careful to leave room for Wendy's car beside hers.

It was still surprising, the little surge of happiness she felt every time driving down the hill into Bittoes, this scattering of houses along the thin prong of land between the inlet and the sea. Even after all these years, knowing the place so well, even despite the work and the irritation lurking in the days ahead, the drive into Bittoes still gave rise to a fresh holiday feeling in her.

A misleading feeling this time. She got out and looked up: the house loomed above, high on its poles, its murky olive weatherboards blurring into the surrounding bush and the pale sky. The wooden stairs zigzagged from the driveway all the way up, stopping twice at broad square landings where you could catch your breath before going on. The two decks stuck out at contrasting angles—a small triangular one for the master bedroom on the upper story and a large one wrapping the whole way around the lower floor. Even from here she could see that the doors along the deck were closed and the blinds down, that Adele was not here. She'd promised to get the early train but clearly had not. Situation normal. Jude was irritated and at the same time somehow gratified that she knew Adele so well.

Up the steep right-hand edge of the block ran the rusting inclinator track.

Standing here on the driveway, you could not see the water for the houses and gardens below, but you could hear it, slapping against the seawall in lazy, rhythmic sloshes. There came the faint whine of an outboard and other motorized noises—leaf blowers across the bay, lawn mowers, vacuuming in a house down the block. Holidaymakers or the people who served them getting ready for Christmas. The humid air smelled of the bay, salty and fishy.

Jude went back and forth, ferrying her bags and boxes of groceries to the inclinator, stacking them on the rusting metal platform. She locked the car, pressing the matte black nugget in her hand, then stepped onto the platform. It swayed with her weight.

The story went that when Sylvie first bought the place in the eighties, even the agent didn't notice the inclinator, overgrown by lantana vine. So for months Sylvie had hauled her things breathlessly up and down the endless stairs. Gail was the one who found it, still operational, and had to teach Sylvie—raised in Melbourne, where it was too flat for need of such a thing—how to use it. The first time Sylvie rode it, she clutched the railing, screeching with delight all the way to the top (**It's a monorail!**), as if she were on a fairground ride.

Jude hated the creaking thing, always had, and avoided it for as long as she could. But with her back now, the stairs had been near impossible for some time. She drew the little chain across behind her and hooked it closed—as if that would do anything to save you. The control panel was like something from a 1950s cartoon spaceship, the fat button loose in its decaying rubber casing. She pushed it and waited. It was always a shock when after a moment the thing actually worked—the platform jolted and began to move. She felt herself levitating, rising slowly past the first stairs. She turned and faced the trees, holding tight to the flimsy metal railings, not looking down as the platform rose up the steep, scrubby incline. Even so she had visions of the rusted metal collapsing, hurling her to the rocks and the bushes. And nobody there to know.

The bay glittered beyond the trees, but she could not look for longer than an instant, willing the trundling, precarious ascension to end. When it did, the inclinator jerked to a stop so sharply she almost overbalanced. She undid the chain and stepped quickly across the gap to the solid deck boards.

The key was in its place under the Buddha head in the corner of the deck, beside the big fishpond barrel. She peered in; the water was low and greasy-looking, but the plants were alive, just. Could any goldfish possibly still be alive in that water?

Which of them had been here last? Not her, and not Adele—Liz didn't like Bittoes and apparently had a strange animosity toward this house. Wendy maybe, here to work on the never-ending book? Certainly Wendy would never think to fill the fishpond.

Jude dragged the hose from the back of the house near the laundry and turned it on, shoving the nozzle to the base of the barrel. Filthy water swirled into life. She didn't stay looking; she did not want to see the desiccated white bellies of dead fish rolling to the surface.

Was it possible that nobody had been here since Sylvie died?

The glimpse of disturbed water, its rising flecks of black sludge, made her uneasy. Which was ridiculous. She waited till the pond was full, turned off the tap, and tugged at the hose. As it fell slithering from the pond, she had a drugged recall of waking from a colonoscopy years ago. Not unpleasant but strange, the slippery flicker of the tubing leaving her body, then her consciousness surrendering to sedation once more.

She pushed the key into the lock.

Inside the house the air was so hot it made her gasp. The living room was a dark cave, and there was a strong moldy smell. She moved to the windows and drew open the curtains, clacking on their heavy wooden rings along the rails. Sunlight streamed into the room. She had to wrench at the bolts and shove the glass doors, stiff on their hinges, before dragging them wide open, pushing a heavy wooden outdoor chair against each to hold them in place.

When she turned back into the room, she found herself facing the wide white sofa she'd given Sylvie not long before she got ill. It was still beautiful. It wasn't white, it was ivory. Jude sank down into it, running her fingers over the fabric of the arms. There were trails of silk glistening through the weave, threads of spiderweb in the rain. She sat in the beautiful sofa, looking around at the dingy room. A shame, how Sylvie's tacky, worn-out things detracted from the sofa's elegance. The puffy armchairs with their cracked tan leather, varnish worn off the wooden arms, and the chunky oak table with its dings and scratches. The horizontal pine paneling at the south end of the room looked more orange than golden now.

What this place needed was a complete overhaul—you'd start with white paint, toss all the junk—but none of that mattered now, because it wasn't Sylvie's place anymore, it was Gail's, and soon it would be someone else's altogether.

Jude stood. Moving through the house, she was visited by the thick silence that settled inside her those few times she had stepped inside a church door. It was possible she was the first to walk these rooms since Sylvie had died.

What did that mean?

Nothing, that's what. Except a lot of work, an empty house full of rubbish that had to be cleared. And Jude, as usual, was the only one to arrive on time, as she'd promised.

She got busy. She snapped up roller blinds, pushing windows open wide, and unlocked each pair of warped glass doors in the living room and bedrooms. Some of the frames were swollen; you always had to shove and drag at the doors if they hadn't been opened for a while.

She stood in the living room, considering for a moment, and then took her own bags into the bedroom at the back, with its window shaded by the close-pressing rock. The house was built into a great curve of sandstone, and it seemed the damp had gotten worse with the place closed for so long. She thought of the airy master bedroom above, its magnificent view. If Adele had arrived first, there was no doubt at all she would have installed herself in there without even pretending to wait to offer it to the others. Most of the time Adele was like a four-year-old at a birthday party; she tried to behave well at first, to suppress her need, but would yield almost instantly to the desire to snatch and grasp.

It was beneath Jude to be that way.

With difficulty she shunted the sticky aluminum window open, along its tracks. The insect screen undulated; she hoped there were no holes—the mosquitoes were worst back here, in the dank air—but she couldn't see properly without her glasses. She sniffed. The room would air out soon enough. Leaving the door open wide, she went back to the living room. Sylvie and Gail's things were there, the same as always. Books in the bookshelf, the trays and vases and that dusty bent peacock feather . . .

Where on earth were the others?

Jude felt a quick plume of anger. Of course Adele was late. But Wendy, too, more than an hour overdue now! **been delayed,** her text had simply said. **there around 1**. Jude had a creeping understanding that Wendy's secrecy must have something to do with the wretched dog. Surely, **surely** she would know he must be left at home, in a kennel, wherever. You could get dog babysitters now, apparently. She shuddered at the thought of anyone having to stay in Wendy's Lewisham house. Dark, musty with dog stink, every surface arrayed with either piles of gritty paper or dirty old dog things: plastic bucket beds, stained cushions, even revolting plastic "doggy steps" so the poor creature could get himself onto the towel-covered couch.

If you went to Wendy's house these past few years—Jude herself avoided it—you had to hold your breath for the smell.

She paused for a moment, running her fingers once more along the back of the sofa (which really was in such good condition she couldn't remember why she'd ever wanted to be rid of it), and then turned in to the kitchen and began unpacking the grocery bags on the countertop. She made another laborious trip to the car, down and up on the inclinator. She had brought the minimum—coffee, bread, eggs, good salt and oil, aged vinegar, milk, a few salad things. An expensive pasture-raised chicken. But Daniel had sent, excessively, a dozen bottles of very nice wine and two of champagne for their holiday. She'd had to split them into separate boxes, and they were still awkward to lift from the car to the inclinator. Once at the top, she had to stoop and drag the boxes along.

Daniel had said he was glad she'd spend this Christmas with the others. He never liked her being alone on holidays. She'd laughed. “I’ve been alone my whole life,” she’d said without rancor.

It was just the truth, the choice they both had made.

Once she’d imagined that they might be together for a single Christmas in Rome; she imagined the moon and bright stars shining through the Pantheon’s oculus at midnight. They hadn’t gone. But sometimes she still thought about it.

“And anyway,” she’d said again to Daniel, “this isn’t a holiday.”

She’d come to this house every December for decades. Sylvie and Gail always went to Gail’s spinster sister in Victor Harbor and left the house for Jude and Daniel. Way back at the start, when what was between them remained a terrifying, thrilling secret, she and Daniel had stayed in the boat shed at the bottom of Marty Faber’s place—one room, smelling of mangrove mud, a tiny double bed where she and Daniel would languish on hot, mosquito-bitten afternoons as the inlet water lapped beneath the floorboards. The smell of mosquito spray took her straight there, even now. And baby oil. They ate Balmain bug tails grilled on the hibachi in the open doorway, eaten with hunks of bread and Jude's herbed mayonnaise.

They'd been so young! All she needed then was a whisk and a knife, a cooler full of ice, seafood, and wine. They left the aluminum espresso pot and the little gas ring in the shed. She didn't ask what the understanding between Marty and Daniel was around that time. She didn't ask about many things in the subsequent thirty-seven years. Jude's life depended on an opaque acceptance of many facets of Daniel's life. The boat shed was romantic but also stultifyingly hot, and no amount of insect coils kept away the clouds of mosquitoes. As big as fucking bats, Daniel used to say. So at some point Sylvie's house—which still had mosquitoes but not so many and at least a fridge and a stove—became her Christmas bolt-hole.

The whole area had morphed and changed several times since those days.

The winding narrow roads were now more likely to be traveled by BMWs and Lexuses than by the surfers' wagons and camper vans of back then. The freeway upgrade meant the trip from Sydney shrank from three or four hours to one and a half on a good day, and the real estate prices had gone berserk. The artists and writers, film people and theater types who could afford shacks here when Bittoes was isolated and cheap now found themselves sitting on gold mines, and those (very) few whose careers had astonishingly taken off, who became famous, lent the place a kind of bohemian celebrity chic.

There were still a few of the original clapboard cottages around, but hardly any remained untouched. Those ones, faded butter yellow or spearmint, were mottled with mold and spiderwebs, hidden in gardens thick with frangipani and insects and thorny hibiscus, but most of the others had been tastefully restored and repaired, painted charcoal and white with red trim or deep blue and green and aqua.

But even these were going. Gradually almost all of them were demolished and replaced by the great glass-and-steel-and-stone monuments like Marty Faber's new place: jagged towers built into the bushy hillsides, elaborate constructions climbing up and ever up, to command views of both the inlet and the sea. These people drove Range Rovers and had their coffee machines plumbed in.

Now the Bittoes populace existed in two cultures, with a shared illusion of honest simplicity. City bankers and surgeons and copyright lawyers who liked to pretend they didn't care about money would flirt with the barmaids at the little weatherboard ex-servicemen's club, mixing it with the fishermen who smoked too much dope and made bawdy jokes decades out of date. The old hippie types, the long-timers, would shake their heads wryly at how mad the land values had gone since they first bought "the shack." They liked to reminisce about dragging coolers full of ice up four or five flights of stairs (before the glass elevators and home-delivered groceries) or the era when you couldn't get around to Duskys except by boat. But for all this nostalgia, Bittoes had grown into a short-term and anonymous place. It was a place of expensive come-and-go weekend rentals, a destination for casual assignations, a place where groups of couples holidayed together until either the friendships or the marriages, or both at once, imploded.

But Jude and Daniel endured. They were separate from, above all this.

Every December, Jude stayed here alone for a week or so, and then Daniel arrived every January 3 for their precious annual week of summer.

Helena obviously knew—she had to, the kids, too—but at some time everyone had wordlessly agreed to accept the outlandish premise that Daniel made an annual visit to his elderly cousin Margery, whom Helena hated and hadn't spoken to in forty-six years.

Sylvie's house was where Jude and Daniel could greet each other in gratitude and peace, where they could live serenely together for one week a year, where they would strike out for a day's tough bushwalking in the heat and then spend the rest of the week virtuously recovering, passing the **New Yorker** and gin and tonics and novels back and forth, and sleeping in the afternoons. It was their place to cook together and to eat—simply but well—and to try new wine varietals from small vineyards and sit out on the deck at night and look at the stars through Sylvie's ancient telescope. They sat high above the town and were tender with each other. They spoke lazily about the things that mattered to them both: beauty, art, books, the way the water was lit in the dawn. They were beyond the reach of the ordinary world, and they were happy.

This year everything would be different.

Daniel was coming on Boxing Day, when Helena was leaving for Europe with her sister. He had to fly out to join them on January 4. He and Jude would have eight days.

In the kitchen she put away her things. She checked the ancient coffee machine for water, found herself automatically reaching for the filter handle—all those years in restaurants—and checking the basket. Surprisingly, it was empty of moldy coffee. She rinsed it anyway, turned it over on the tray.

It was lucky she was here first, really. Adele wouldn't have done any of this—filled the fishpond, aired out the rooms, turned on the gas (she wouldn't know how, or even that such things needed to be done).

Jude had kept her thoughts steered carefully away from the fact that this would be the last time here, for her and Daniel. Neither had mentioned it. They'd find somewhere else, doubtless somewhere better. They could find somewhere with a pool, a better kitchen. But something would be lost all the same.

She surveyed Sylvie's kitchen now. The dingy room with its peeling orange laminate countertops, their rounded wooden edges silky with years of being touched, being casually used and disregarded in an absent holiday way and never, she supposed, actually properly cleaned.

She revisited a clandestine thought: if they sold Jude's apartment, that would surely bring more than enough to buy a moldering old house with its flimsy, impractical stairs and rusting inclinator, its proximity to the nature reserve that regularly went up in flames in the summer bushfires that never crossed the boundary fence behind, though almost did several times.

But the selling and buying of property was not her realm—she had no interest in it, and anyway this was just sentimentality. She knew she couldn't live here, not really. What would she do in the drizzling winters? She would shrivel with boredom. There was no proper heating. But it wasn't just that—the long days away from the city with no bookshops, no lectures at the library or symphony concerts. She tried to picture herself here, her own lovely pieces around her, the place whitewashed and scrubbed clean. But all she could see was the surrounding bush pressing in, the hard reflective water far below. Jude had no illusions, but something unpleasant threatened if she followed these thoughts.

She opened the narrow pantry's doors and saw with satisfaction that inside it was filthy. It would take a long afternoon's work to clear it out.

And then she heard the rumble of the inclinator motor. Beyond the window she saw the little platform jolt into life, begin its empty descent.

Wendy had to bend double on the wretched contraption to hold Finn still, trying to stop his claws scrabbling over the metal edge of the platform as it moved, and he gave out terrified sounds of distress in his hoarse old bark all the way up. At the top he scrambled beneath the chain to leap onto the deck and then tottered around, dazed with fear, while Wendy unloaded her bags. She would have to do another trip for the rest of Finn's things in a minute.

"Helloo!" she called, carrying her squashy cooler bag of fridge bits and pieces indoors, dumping it on the counter.

"Finally!" Jude's voice called back, trying to sound as if she were joking.

Wendy looked around to find Jude on her knees at the pantry, a grubby rubbish bin beside her. She tossed a few more things into it with vigorous urgency before laboriously making her way upright. It was probably unfair of Wendy to suspect that this delay was a performance, to punish her for being late. The garish yellow rubber gloves were especially ridiculous, as if handling dusty spice bottles and cans of kidney beans were somehow hazardous, toxic work. Jude came toward her now, smiling with the tight friendliness that showed she was already annoyed. When they got near enough to embrace, Jude reared back.

"Oh, yes, sorry, dog piss," said Wendy, wafting the air before her with both hands.

"The car broke down. We had to wait an hour and a **half** for the man to come and fix it!"

A great exhaustion was swamping her now. It was so hot. For a moment she expected sympathy, to be offered a glass of water, but this was Jude.

"Dear God," Jude said. "You'll have to change those clothes. And he **has** to stay outside, Wendy."

Wendy nodded, looking around the kitchen at Sylvie's things—battered tin canisters, a cracked white teapot. A thickness came into her throat. "It's so strange. It's just exactly the same."

Jude looked for a moment as though she, too, might feel this sadness. But she made only a grunt that meant **What did you expect?** and turned back to her cupboard, her important, interrupted work.

Finn was already pacing back and forth along the deck when Wendy did her second trip with the inclinator, carrying the dog's bedding in her arms. She made a little nest out of the big tartan cushion and some towels in the far corner where there was some dappled shade and tied another towel across the railings as a makeshift awning. But he refused to lie down or sit. He only limped up and down the boards. Up and down, then around and around.

Jude's disapproval sounded from the house with the irregular thumping of food cans into the plastic bin.

Wendy sat down heavily at the outdoor table, breathless with the effort of all that had already gone wrong, and called, pointlessly, to Finn.

After a little while, Jude emerged from indoors with a peace offering—a glass of cold water for Wendy and a decaying red plastic ice cream container of water for Finn. She set it down at the edge of the deck and summoned him in a cold, gruff voice: "Come on, then, you silly animal."

Finn did not move or register the sound of her voice but stood by the railing, staring at nothing. "He's deaf, remember," Wendy said. She moved to the bowl and bent down to place herself in Finn's line of sight, calling to him sweetly. When he saw her he emerged from his trance, limped slowly across the deck toward the bowl, not reaching it but stopping a foot away, staring into the air again. Wendy encouraged him with a low, soft crooning, dragging him closer to the bowl by the collar, then gently turning his face to point at the bowl. "Water, drink," said Wendy.

But Finn seemed frightened by the bowl and lurched backward. He began a slow, painful-looking walk away from them, then looked as if he would return but instead sat up tall, erect, motionless as stone. Then, infinitesimally slowly, his body began to curve inward until he could no longer stay upright, and he sank to the boards, asleep.

"Oh, for God's sake," said Jude.

"Where's Adele?" Wendy asked, to distract her.

"I've no idea," Jude said crisply. She wrung out a cloth over the railing, wrenching it in both hands. "But she can get a taxi from the station. I haven't got time to go collect her now, there's too much to do." And she went back inside, letting the screen door smack loudly closed behind her.

Jude the martyr, Jude the boss. It made Wendy feel tired, to think of the days to come. All she wanted to do, like Finn, was to lie down and sleep.

Passing through the living room, she came across the enormous white couch. Still new looking, sumptuous, utterly incongruous in the room. Only Jude, whose clean-lined apartment was filled with fine, pale ceramics and rich-people designer furniture, would have a thing like this to give away.

Doubtless the couch was to do with Daniel. His castoff, or he'd given Jude some other expensive replacement. Every time you went to her place, it looked somehow different. Daniel's money was a steady, generous tide, washing up new things, taking old ones away. It seemed that was enough for Jude.

The sofa was certainly beautiful. You

did want to lie down here, to push yourself into its softness and sleep. Wendy lowered herself into its folds and at last felt her body release into rest. She looked around and saw with great fondness the same old room. Sylvie's pictures, Sylvie's things. It was the same lovely, simple house. But now, around the bright sofa, it looked dusty and shabby. Wendy felt insulted on Sylvie's behalf. It had been wrong of Jude to impose her taste, her wealth, on Sylvie's house. Something had been, was still being, spoiled by it. It was strange to Wendy that now, after all these years, the affair with Daniel—about which Jude had always been so secretive—should begin to leak into visibility, here in Sylvie's house.

Wendy traced a silk curlicue on the arm of the sofa with her finger. Through the glass doors, she could see Finn sound asleep on the boards at the end of the deck, legs flopped out to one side, tail limp. He was so utterly still he might have died there, finally, in the heat and the smudges of shade. The fur had worn off his elbows and shins, and his blotchy pink skin showed through. She watched his chest, his face, for movement. At last she saw a tiny movement at his throat, the faintest swell of his belly. He swallowed, breathed, lived.

CHAPTER THREE

Adele had hoped most people would get off at Hornsby, but new passengers streamed into the carriage instead, hauling suitcases and shouldering shopping bags along the aisles. Adele left her overnight bag on the seat beside her, its quilted red bulk reassuring. She could hardly put it on the floor; it wouldn't fit. And the floor was sticky, as train floors always were. She peered serenely out the window while people shuffled past her, choosing other seats. A pair of students sat heavily down in front of her, murmuring seriously to each other in Chinese. They had not seen the Quiet Carriage sign. Someone would scold them soon enough.

The train moved off, the platform and buildings sliding by, the soft blue sky opening above. There was an odd smell coming from somewhere. The air in the carriage was oppressive despite the feeble air-conditioning.

Adele hadn't specially chosen the quiet carriage, but now she was glad of it, of the peaceable respect that lay between the passengers, the lullaby rocking of the carriage over the tracks. It was one of the older trains, and its lurch and sway were calming, after what had happened. The journey would be another hour at least from here, and the seats were high-backed, better suited to these longer trips than the new suburban trains. She watched the olive bushland whirring by. Added to everything else, there was the specter of Jude's displeasure at her tardiness hanging over the hours ahead. Adele wasn't even brave enough to text her, not yet.

The students had stopped talking, and in the new stillness she felt something looming. When she looked up, a woman was standing in the aisle, rocked gently by the train's movement, staring coldly at Adele's bag but saying nothing. Adele made a surprised, apologetic cluck, as if she had realized only this instant that there were no other free spaces in the carriage and that her own bag was taking up a whole seat. She wrestled it to the floor, puffing a little to make obvious the difficulty of the exercise.

The woman did not acknowledge Adele as she rammed in her own square suitcase, forcing Adele to squash her legs even closer to the wall. The woman was about Adele's own age, maybe older, with dull brown hair in a poorly cut style, too short to be pretty but not short enough for a statement. She dug around in her handbag on her lap and drew out a silver transistor radio with a little single earbud, which she screwed into her ear. A transistor! Adele almost snorted: Did this woman **want** people to know how old she was? She leaned farther into the window, resting her arm along the wide sill. A moment later she sneaked another glance, surprised to realize that despite the gray showing through her fading dye job, the woman could actually be a bit younger than Adele was herself; she could be sixty-five, even. It was easy to examine her, hunched over a book of sudoku puzzles, oblivious to Adele's inspection.

She wore wire rimmed glasses halfway down her nose, held a red felt pen in her fingers. Sudoku books and transistors, dear God. And when Adele leaned down to retrieve her own handbag, she saw flesh-colored stocking socks over the thin ankles. Mushy floral trousers, navy senior-citizen sandals.

The pantyhose made Adele feel a bit sick.

The smell lingered in the carriage. It was a stale smell, coming from old hot chips perhaps, overlaid with some other sweeter, artificial scent, like American doughnuts. But also, and more strongly now, there was an unpleasant antiseptic smell, as if someone had been sick nearby and someone else had cleaned it up. There was a trace of sourness under the disinfectant smell. Someone always had to clean up—Adele knew that more than anybody.

She'd missed the first two trains to Bittoes, sitting there on the platform at Central. She couldn't go, could not face Jude and Wendy. By the time she'd realized she had no choice—where else could she go, at Christmas?—she'd had to wait another hour for the next one.

The woman scribbled in her sudoku book. In a little while, she wriggled to unbuckle her sandals, and then Adele heard her scratch one ankle with the toe of her other foot.

She imagined telling Sylvie, the two of them snickering. "Pantyhose": what a word. **Scritch, scritch** went the nylon stockings.

At home Sylvie grinned from the front of

the booklet on Adele's side of the bed, her wry, amused eyes gazing straight out. The spotted blue kerchief tied jauntily around her head. Liz would never come out and say that she thought this a maudlin, a macabre thing to do, keeping it there on the bedside table so long after the funeral. But Adele just wanted to see Sylvie's face. It was odd, how often you didn't have photographs of those you loved the most. Sylvie would have been baffled if Adele wanted to take her photo, even just with her phone. **What** for? she would have said. She didn't have a clue what Instagram even was.

Adele took out her phone, steering her thoughts away from Sylvie, as she had learned to do, before the deep, painful heave of missing began. The understanding was still seeping in that she must steer away from Liz now, too.

She had a look at Twitter, then Instagram, saw that @adele_antoniactress had 734 followers now. Was that more or less than before? There were three new comments.

OMG I love you, with five bouquet emojis. **Hey, I'm making animations and would appreciate it if you would visit my Instagram page And my Cartoons . . .** and then: **So cute!!! Love your lines!** with three lipstick kisses.

Love your lines. She supposed she couldn't report that as an offensive comment. The screen froze; reception had dropped out again. She flipped the phone cover shut.

The sudoku woman let out a deep, soft burp. Adele twisted around in her seat to let her disgust be known, but the woman merely kept on with her puzzle, unperturbed. Adele exhaled audibly and closed her eyes for a second, eyebrows high, hoping the woman might notice her **dear God** expression.

It was all too much. The smell, the woman, Jude's moods to come, Liz, all the things she had to consider now. Like the contents of her bank account, which she would have to face in a minute.

But in two days it would be Christmas,

and that was soothing. Whenever Adele thought of Christmas, it was with pleasure, like a child. She'd always felt this way. Everyone rolled their eyes now about Christmas, spoke of it with contempt. They were exhausted at the thought; they complained about consumerism and environmental degradation—all that plastic and tinsel, choking fish. They disapproved of the excess, so much waste it was obscene. Who on earth wanted presents at this age? (Adele did!) It was somehow juvenile to look forward to Christmas, but she couldn't help it. It made her think of beautiful thick paper to unwrap, the smell of pine needles. It made her think of festive, glossy things: cherries, baubles, jelly. What was wrong with that?

The train slithered over its tracks. Now and then someone's phone—not hers—let out a loud ping or pong, causing heads to rise in irritation.

She was not going to be allowed Christmas this year. They'd be at Bittoes to **work,** Jude had kept telling her unnecessarily. Still, Jude would surely make her pavlova. She made it each year for the lunch before the holidays, before everyone went their separate ways. Jude's meringue was like sharp snow, and she piled the thick cream disgracefully high with raspberries and soaked plums of some kind, and in recent years she had added the beveled stars of pomegranate seeds. The pavlova was essential. A tradition.

Take anything you want, Gail had said.

Adele was consoled for a moment by this; perhaps there might be some surprise, some little gift for her from Sylvie beyond the grave, even though Sylvie wouldn't have known she was leaving it. Jude would make beautiful food despite herself, certainly the pavlova. And Wendy would be disorganized and breathless, for she was getting fatter all the time, it seemed, and Adele would be able to feel sorry for her. In fact, it would be possible to feel quite wealthy for a couple of days with nothing to spend money on, lying on daybeds, sinking her bare feet into Sylvie's thick rugs. She would lick whipped cream from her fingers.

Last year Jude had scattered quartered figs over the luscious red pile on top of the meringue. This was a week after Adele's first kiss with Liz, and she had not yet told her friends. But the figs, lying there so shameless and open, had caused a new squirming inside her as she slipped one into her mouth.

There was no point thinking about any of this now. This year no lunch and no Christmas. And after that . . . she blinked hard, to banish the tears that could come if she let them.

The faint vomity smell came again, stray wispy ribbons of unpleasant air. Someone always had to clean up. But what if you didn't know where the mess was?

The train was at full speed now, the rural fringe of the city whizzing past in a monochromatic blur: streaky blue sky, scrubby trees and bush. She saw birds burst from trees as the train passed. The branches swung, faltered, and Adele once more pushed away this morning's moment with Liz. She didn't even know, she realized now, what the mess was.

She let her shoulders drop down and back, drew her navel toward her spine. Let the invisible thread at her crown lift her head from her neck, separate the vertebrae. So many women hunched and slouched. That was all right when you were twenty and thin as a stick, when you could drape yourself over any old thing, when looking sleepy and louche and amenable was beautiful. But now, no. It was more of a turtle look that many of her friends had now, chins forward, heads low. Or worse, a **widow's hump.** What a horrible expression. She sneaked another glance at the woman. Gratifyingly, there was the definite hint of a widow's hump.

Adele knew hardly any widows except Wendy, which was surprising at their age. Divorce didn't count, even if your ex-husband was long dead (poor Ray with his heart attack, but he'd been a bastard, so . . .). And Jude's situation . . . well, what would that be called? "Mistress" meant young.

Adele sat tall in her seat and allowed her neck to lengthen, looking around the carriage as she did. She landed her soft smile on a man and woman a few rows behind her. The woman was showing her phone to the man, saying, **See?** But he stared straight back at Adele. Aggressively, she felt. Huge, blocky head, bald and stone-like. A large Band-Aid was taped over his nose, covering part of his right cheek. It made him look hostile, even violent.

Adele turned back around, wishing she hadn't smiled. Perhaps he'd just had a skin cancer cut away and was not violent. But his eyes were cold when he stared at her. Yet she was just being friendly to fellow travelers. At Christmas! She was sick of the quiet carriage now; a little festive chatter would be more cheerful. She hoped they would all get off at the next station—the violent man, the pantyhose woman. There was nobody of Adele's kind here in the carriage, probably not even on the whole train.

Well, **c'est la vie.** That was nothing new. She closed her eyes, resumed her Pilates posture, concentrated on allowing the softening of her face, her throat.

Hostility had followed Adele her whole life, she thought tolerantly. She'd always been an outsider—all artists were. The thing she'd done that was unforgivable was to stay in the theater while other people got proper jobs. She'd spent her life living **all** the parts of herself, while normal people lived along the slenderest, most limited path of experience. They did not know themselves in the least. She made art, not money; and that, like slouching, was all right when you were young. Artistic poverty was romantic when you were thirty. It was after fifty that people began despising you for it.

She'd dreamed about Jimmy last night. It happened sometimes, even now. She couldn't remember what was in the dream. Probably just being his big sister, holding his hand.

When she was young and starting out

in the theater, Jimmy's criminality—his violence—lent her a kind of glamour; men particularly seemed to like it. Ray especially. But visiting jail wasn't like people thought. The truth was, there was nothing interesting about jail—that was clear immediately. After a few years, she stopped going altogether; she couldn't stand the boredom of it any longer. And then Jimmy died and it wasn't dramatic, it was lymphoma at forty-eight, and she didn't feel guilty even when she inspected the sad little collection of his belongings: a plastic watch, his pharmacy prescriptions, a pair of smelly sneakers—all of which she threw into the bin. They didn't have a funeral, but she did still have the dreams here and there.

She took up her phone now that the network was back and tapped the banking app again. The Airbnb money could not, she knew rationally, be there until after Christmas—the day after Boxing Day at the earliest. But she just needed to check, in case it came early. That would be a welcome surprise, if it came early. Or perhaps there would be some other, unexpected little windfall. Very occasionally this still happened. Perhaps there had been another rerun of **Boronia Street** in Slovenia or some other similarly benevolent country, screening late at night, dubbed with strange voices.

As the little red wheel on her phone screen slowly turned—**We are logging you in**—she caught sight of her new sandals, the pleasing hot pink polish gleaming on her toenails. She looked around again and confirmed that in this carriage, perhaps in the whole train, all colors were muted and dull except for the bright figure of Adele. If you came into this carriage—if you were a normal sort of person, not like Pantyhose—you would be cheered by the vibrant sight of Adele Antoniades, her freshly colored, rich blond hair twisted into its familiar stylish knot, the crimson linen smock falling pleasantly over those (frankly, still terrific) breasts, her lips pink and glossy.

The network vanished, the bank app froze once more. Adele looked at her feet, flexed her toes. She liked the beading and the tiny white shells sewn into the sandal leather, liked seeing her tanned feet beneath the white capri pants. The sandals had been on sale; they were the kind that made you think of Bali, of gleaming stone floors in expensive tropical hotels. She had paid for the mani-pedicure with the contents of the ceramic cup on the counter—she had found sixty-eight dollars in there, in coins! She'd emptied the cup onto a tea towel on the table while Liz was out. Not that Liz would care at all. Adele could not say exactly what it was that made her not want to be seen emptying the change jar. The zipper of her little fabric purse had strained as she drew it closed around the lumpy contents.

The app finally opened. The money had not come in. There wasn't any windfall.

Instead the phone buzzed with a message from Jude: **where ARE you??**

The pension—another hated word—had

already gone for this month. A sudden urge to cry now forced its way painfully up her chest, and she inhaled so audibly to stop it that even Pantyhose glanced her way. She pulled a tissue from her sleeve and smiled, shook her head, pretending an aborted sneeze. The woman turned back to her puzzle, uninterested in Adele.

She would not be able to tell Jude or Wendy about the conversation with Liz, for she felt obscurely ashamed. It had been the kind of remark that made Adele feel stupid and in some way unclean. What Liz had said, in a careful voice, was that when Adele got back, they would need to have a talk. Adele, smiling there with her red suitcase packed, waiting for the Uber driver booked by Liz to take her to the station, had been momentarily baffled. She had no idea what Liz was talking about, but in a flash she knew it had something to do with Milly's suddenly very potent stillness in the next room—she knew that this moment had been discussed, planned. Rehearsed, even, daughter coaching mother.

"Back" was the word Liz had used. She didn't say when you get "home." And right then Adele knew she must leave Liz's house immediately, and that she could never return. She'd stood smiling stupidly at Liz, who did not meet her eye, and then Liz walked her to the Uber and patted the car door, and her face wore a strange look—relief, pride?—as she said, "Merry Christmas, Del." They didn't kiss. And then Adele had been carried by Liz's credit card to the train station and deposited there, where she'd sat dumbfounded on a seat, missing trains and trying to understand what had happened.

She felt afraid now of the days to come with Jude and Wendy, together in Sylvie's rotting old house that had to be cleaned. They would not have Christmas, the Airbnb money had not come in, and she did not know what the mess was or how she'd made it, but she knew it meant she was alone again now.

She stared out the window, and she felt the familiar fear crawling toward her through the long gray corridors of the train. She'd seen them on two or three television reports now. It was an issue, **a growing epidemic,** the homelessness of older women. She watched these foolish, acquiescent women, exposing themselves on national television. Offering their small, ashamed smiles to reporters while they tried to explain—unsatisfactorily, hopelessly—how things had come to this. Wearing their cheap clothes and lipstick for the camera, picking at their nails, smiling in that desperate way, showing the journalist with a weird sort of pride how they showered in campgrounds and did their makeup in department store restrooms. Women who'd once been safe, and loved, but who had not been careful with money, who had not paid attention. Who'd hoped things would get better, somehow. First they stayed with friends, with their children, but then things happened, things got worse. And now they lived in their cars, cast unwanted into the ugly suburbs.

Adele didn't even have a car.

But she had herself. She wanted to shout, to stand in the carriage to make a crazed speech: **I have gifts, talents!** The woman beside her no doubt had a car. Pantyhose and a transistor and a car, probably an investment property as well as her own brick town house. Probably a retirement fund, vast sums tucked away earning interest. A sluice of awful clarity washed through Adele: she had wasted her life waiting for her tide to turn, while other people—people who cared nothing for art, or literature, who had probably never even seen a single Shakespeare play—these people, in the end, were victorious. They did not live out their old age sleeping in cars, pretending to have picnics in the park every night of their lives.

Oh, please.

That was Sylvie's voice. And then Adele saw her new sandals again, the shell beads, her gleaming toenails. She was not there yet. The others would help her out, just for the moment. And then something would turn up. It always had. Fear was fuel; every actress knew that. She straightened in her seat and put her shoulders back, and the train slid out into an open patch of air. The shocking silver glory of the Hawkesbury River beneath her, a mirror for the bright, clear sky above.

Wendy made her bed—Jude had decreed that they must bring their own bedlinens, there wouldn't be time for laundry—and then sat on it in the damp air. They'd both left the upstairs room for Adele. She didn't know why, except that they always did. Somehow, over time, the unspoken understanding had grown that they—Jude, Sylvie, Wendy—were the adults and Adele was the child. Struck by it now, Wendy wasn't sure when or how this had come about. When they first met in their thirties, Adele had been mighty: She held entire theaters in her thrall, commanding from the stage. She shone from newspaper pages, was beamed at in the streets by strangers. She was on television (quality drama only), had significant parts in serious films: Bruce Beresford, Fred Schepisi. But mainly she lived on the stage, she was an artist. Her face filled theater posters at bus stops.

But now . . . well, Wendy couldn't say when exactly it had changed, but she knew that if she took the good room and Adele was left this one, with its poky dimensions and the smell of mildew, there would be injured glances and meaningful, somehow servile silences, and Adele had already sounded strange on the phone, and for her entire life Wendy had been too tired for dramatics.

She liked this room anyway, with its squeaky metal bed frame, despite the slight moldy feeling already starting in her chest. The bed was familiar and soft. She had lain on it so many times with Sylvie on past holidays and weekends, propped on their elbows discussing their lives while Lance went out fishing or shopping for groceries with Gail. They would lie here snorting with laughter or indignation or drifty with pleasant boredom, or Wendy would sit cross-legged on the floor with a mug of tea or a gin glass while Sylvie draped herself over the bed, complaining about Gail, or her work, or being fat. Sometimes they would share a joint, passing it back and forth, catching ash in their hands. Wendy could not think of the last time she'd been able to sit cross-legged on the floor and get up by herself. And smoking a joint! That would be lovely, except her lungs already flinched at the thought.

Where was Finn? She was suddenly alert: if he got inside, Jude would be on the warpath. She peeked outside, but he wasn't there, not asleep in his bed, nor had he wandered down the side of the house. She came inside, moved quickly, furtively through the empty rooms.

The toilet, of course. There he was, motionless, his face hovering between the wall and the back of the toilet. Once he got into such a spot, he could not find his way out again; reversing was beyond him now. He would simply wait patiently for her to come and find him.

"Come on, darling," she whispered now, pulling at his collar. He jerked when she touched him and skidded a little on the floor. But she sat on the closed toilet lid and gradually maneuvered him around, pushing and pulling, until he sat at her feet. They rested quietly in the dark, tiled space for a moment. Jude, mercifully, could still be heard bustling and clanking in the kitchen. Wendy remembered something odd: many years ago, in her fifties, she sat on the toilet one day, and as she pissed, she thought, **I smell like my grandmother.** It was shocking: that there was a smell, that she recognized it, that it was her body, that it was to do with growing older. She'd quickly finished and washed her hands and hurried out, and she had never thought of it again until this moment.

Finn sat on the lumpy brown-tiled floor,

his mottled belly swelling and subsiding with each shallow breath. Lost in his blurry inner world.

"Come on, Finny," she whispered, though she knew he could not hear, and he limped along behind her through the rooms, the two of them silently making their way out toward the air and light, the trees and the sky.

The taxi looped around the hairpin bends, down the bushy hillsides into Bittoes. Adele sniffed the salty air and twisted in the backseat to look into the open doorway of the small gift shop on the corner as they passed.

She could work in a little gallery shop like that. The affluent suburbs were crawling with little chichi places like it, the kind of place with discreet, modern jewelry wound around bits of wood, wispy scarves in the colors of nature. And ceramics, glossy on the inside and matte on the exterior. Perhaps a pair or two of sneakers in black and taupe, a couple of enormous cushions on the floor.

Fancy gardening gloves, that type of thing.

There would be lots of places, in fact, where Adele Antoniades would be welcome doing this sort of work, talking to customers—she was charming, her face was familiar! She would be a drawing card. **Oh, thank you,** she would murmur, wrapping a pair of silk socks in extravagant layers of tissue paper. Very modest. **Oh, no, I've been working on other projects for a while.** She would hint at some entrepreneurial thing, something womanly, innovative. In the wellness industry, perhaps . . . She saw herself—subdued makeup, hair pulled back—gracefully busy behind a curving wooden counter. They didn't even have cash registers, these places, which was a bonus. Just subtle little drawers built into the table where you found big white sheets of paper and a few pens and you wrote out the sale on a receipt pad with carbon paper. She would wear black, very simple—or no, charcoal. With some stylish sleeve detail but fitted so that you could see her figure, which was still really very lovely. People said that to Adele often. **You have a lovely figure.** Which meant, **You have terrific tits. For your age.**

A filament of disquiet floated across Adele's vision: there would have to be a credit card machine. But how difficult could that be? She remembered the fish-shop girl's face at her last week as she muttered, **Don't press it twice,** and then the contemptuous sigh, as if Adele were not standing right in front of her, as if she could not see or hear her. But you could just press Cancel and start again. Anyway, she was better with technology than most people. Than Jude and Wendy, certainly.

"Right to the end of this road, thank you so much," she said, leaning forward to speak, bestowing her warmth upon the driver. She lingered a moment, but it was clear he had absolutely no idea who she was. She sat back in her seat. It had been hurtful to realize, sometime ago, that it was only a certain generation to whom the name Adele Antoniades meant anything at all. Some of Liz's friends didn't even know of her, and they were in their fifties. As for Milly, she just looked blank when her mother had boasted—many months ago now, which itself was painful—about Adele's renown. **Awesome,** she'd said, monotone. Milly's nasty little friend Anastasia was soon graduating from the National Institute of Dramatic Arts. At the restaurant table with them all, Adele had waited for Anastasia to ask her for advice, but the girl only shoveled pad thai into her ridiculously huge mouth (Anastasia had been told, Milly reported, that her mouth was **exactly** like Jessica Chastain's) and prattled away in that grating voice about agents and scouts and moving to L.A.

Adele soothed herself by returning to the little gallery of her mind. The rustling of tissue, the soft clack of smooth wooden coat hangers. It would have to be flexible hours, as she'd certainly get some voice work in the new year, maybe a TV ad. It was possible. Last week she'd told Lorraine she might be willing to consider the Comfypad lacy thing, even though it was insulting, if they were still offering thirty-five—nobody watched television at that time of day anyway, she reasoned—and only if she could refuse the billboard. But Lorraine replied not to bother; she'd pitched another client for that, but they'd wanted someone younger. Preferably mid- to late forties.

The taxi pulled away, leaving her standing with her bags on the street below Sylvie's house. She heard a baby crying behind her, and when she turned around, it was a lone seagull, the hot breeze ruffling its coat of feathers. It stood on the grass, shrieking at her. She looked at it and thought, **You think** you're **upset.**

CHAPTER FOUR

Jude stared with distaste at Finn, her lurid rubber-gloved forearms clamped across her thin frame as she stood in the laundry doorway.

When Wendy had followed Jude here around the back of the house, he'd staggered to his feet and plodded after them. Now he paced with a slow, awkward gait, as if constantly stepping over some invisible barrier.

"I'll take him for a walk a bit later," said

Wendy lightly. "He'll be too tired after that to pace."

But she looked sorrowfully out at her darling old boy and knew that this was not true. His addled mind was driven by nothing now, it seemed, but this need to keep moving, despite exhaustion, despite everything. His claws were too long; she should have been clipping them, but he got so upset when she tried that she gave up. She recalled the vet nurse—Sharnelle? Janelle?—puffing out admonishments with her cigarette breath as she expertly took hold of Finn and he lay mute in her lap while she demonstrated: **You need to use an emery board. It's the front ones you have to worry about.** But Wendy had tried; she couldn't get near him with an emery board! If she tried to grasp hold of his foot, he howled, terrorized. The children were the same every time she'd tried to cut their fingernails or even brush their hair when they were small. She loved them too much to hurt them. She left such things alone; they'd bite the nails themselves when they got too long. And what were a few fuzzy knots in a child's gossamer hair? Eventually—after too many rounds of nits—Lance took the bull by the horns and carted them off to the hairdresser himself. She couldn't have borne it, the screaming and writhing. Lance was the one for that sort of thing. Thank God.

She let Finn pace and kept a guilty eye on his toenails. She thought they were all right. The limp was arthritis, not toenails, and if he was in real pain he wouldn't be able to pace, she reasoned. The body looked after itself was what Wendy believed. So she let him pace—what else was there to do? It was incessant. The only time he stopped at home was at night, when he slept on Wendy's bed, when he could feel her breathing, slow and evenly, beside him. But there was no way that could happen here; under Jude's watch he would be banished outside for the duration.

It was possible she would need to sleep with him in the dog blankets, out on the deck.

She could give him some of the Valium. But getting the tablets into him was an ordeal she could not think about now, not with Jude right here, pointing out everything to be done in the gloomy cave of the laundry.

From the front of the house, they heard the inclinator grumble into life.

Looking at Sylvie's place, Adele thought it extraordinary now that here was a house, empty, unclaimed. The inclinator was taking an age to descend. She would use it just this once, to bring her suitcase up. After that—use it or lose it—she would take the stairs.

Another thread of a dream's edge from last night came to her, so fleetingly she couldn't grasp it. It had a feeling of delicacy, and luxury, and also of threat.

At last the platform appeared, and she stepped on, pulled the little chain across, and began her ascent. She slowly trundled upward, water glinting through the trees, and her heart lifted: there it was, the bay, its silver tendrils snaking into the inlets and around the curves of bushland. She felt herself alive, here on her small stage moving through the leaves and branches, the salty air turning to menthol, the cicadas growing louder.

Her dearest friends would be here to greet her. For a few days, perhaps, she could hold off the Liz conversation, could suspend herself here in this sanctuary, in the care of her friends.

At the top she stepped off, called hello, and went to the edge of the deck, spreading her arms along the railings and leaning out. From here you could see almost the whole bay. Things were possible, new perspectives could be perceived, at this height. She grasped her suitcase and wheeled it into the house.

Nobody was here to greet her. They

were not in the kitchen, nor the living room, nor the downstairs bedrooms. Adele popped her head into each one. But when she returned to the kitchen, she could hear muffled conversation coming from somewhere. They were out the back, in the laundry.

She shouted to the wall, "Hello! I'm here!"

She waited for them to call back, to hurry in with their arms out to greet her, but there was just a bit of shuffling noise, and then their two weary-sounding voices calling acknowledgment, they'd be out in a minute. There were no shouts of delight; they did not rush into the room. The rising possibility she'd felt outside drained away, and she knew that if they saw her face now, once more on the edge of tears, she would not be able to stop herself confessing, howling, about Liz.

"No rush!" she yelled to the wall, hurrying out of the kitchen. "I'll just put my stuff in my room." And she bumped her suitcase unhappily up the stairs.

• • • •

A short time later, having unpacked a pair of Liz's Egyptian cotton sheets and tucked them over the bed, lying barefoot on the expanse of it beneath the clanking air conditioner, Adele stared at the ceiling and did her sums again. Wendy's little loan would see her through the week. The Airbnb money would surely come in after Boxing Day. Beyond that was a space Adele would not enter. It was another room, one to which the door would be left closed.

She thought of Liz, of the soft warmth of her body across the bed. Tears swelled in her throat, but she swallowed them down. That door, too, would be left closed.

She got up and opened the French doors to the bare triangle of her deck so the heat could come into the air-conditioned room. She suddenly wanted the humidity on her skin, she wanted to be in the world, not separate from it. She stood in the open doorway for a moment and put a tentative foot outside; the wooden boards were hot beneath her foot. She climbed again into the center of the big white bed, staring out at the silver-and-green view.

If you were very rich, nature would be yours to possess. It surrounded you, it was wilderness owned by nobody, and yet by being rich you could have dominion over the bays and the shores; even the streets below you were yours to claim or dismiss, as you wished. You could look down in a peaceable, generous way over all the dull, ugly details . . . the unpaid bills, the leaf blowers, the women who lugged sacks of linen to holidaymakers from house to house, who waddled down driveways in their leggings and baseball caps and T-shirts, carrying buckets, hoisting vacuum hoses over their shoulders.

She had a fleeting, illogical thought: if you were very rich, you did not need to die.

It seemed unfair that Adele had never been rich, not properly. It was another little tributary of disappointment she could dip into if she wished. To be an actress was to hold a permanent ticket in a magnificent global lottery. It was one of the things that kept you going, the fantasy possibility of sudden fame, riches raining down upon you. She'd seen it happen often enough. It could still happen, even later in life (look at Angela Beaumont!). Why should Adele, with all her talents, be kept from its reach?

She curled on her side. She did not want to get old. She did not want to die and be lain on a high metal bed in a hospital viewing room with a gauzy curtain, you dead on one side and your friends alive, afraid, on the other. And now Adele sat up, and she wanted to flee this place. She'd had to come; there was no choice. But there was also no Sylvie, and how could this be?

The thirties were the age you fell most dangerously in love, Adele had discovered, after the fact. Not with a man or a woman but with your friends. Lovers back then came and went like the weather (or were sent away, like Ray when they found out he'd belted her; poor Lance, absolutely petrified but still confronting Ray at his own front door, telling him to pack his stuff and fuck off, the blood draining from his face only after they'd dead-bolted the door and heard the car roar away, and they all sat in silence on the couch). No, it wasn't lovers but friends—these courageous, shining people—you pursued, romanced with dinners and gifts and weekends away. It was so long ago. Forty years! But it was like looking through water; some things were magnified, their colors more intense. It was a vivid, blossoming time. They saw their best selves in one another, meeting at the Waterside, where Jude kept the corner table for them and sent over special little morsels and glasses of champagne. Adele would come in late from the theater, still in her stage makeup, and they'd cheer and open their arms to her, pulling her into their circle. Lance and Wendy, Sylvie and Gail, everybody smoking and laughing and grandly shouting. Jude would eventually drop into a seat beside them and eye a waiter, who immediately brought more champagne.

Jude was no doubt already seeing Daniel even then, gliding between the bar where he sat and their table, then back again. Always holding herself just a little bit separate, even then. Not that any of them noticed; they just adored Jude's cool panache. How had they all come together anyway? Wendy knew Sylvie from Oxford, and Jude's restaurant was a few doors from the theater. . . . Adele couldn't remember how else—did she meet Sylvie at one of Jude's famous parties?—but one by one they were drawn into the current of the others, and they fell in love and stayed there.

But the current had slowly subsided. And they were left drifting.

Adele and Wendy and Jude did not fit properly anymore, without Sylvie. They'd been four, it was symmetrical. When they went on holidays, they shared two hotel rooms, two beds in each. There were four places at the table, two on each side. Now there was an awful, unnatural gap.

She flopped back down on the bed. What she wanted to do this minute was go home and eat and eat and get very fat.

But where **was** home now?

She briefly saw herself, a sophisticated older woman—all right, she could hear Jude's correction, yes, **old,** she was already old—living here on the top floor of Sylvie's house. There would be someone, some eager young person, an actress perhaps, who came to her for advice, for Adele certainly had things to say, about acting, about life. . . . This young actress would bring her meals. She didn't eat much, she'd never eaten much, but she had things to share about the life of an actor that nobody had ever asked her. All the interviews she could have done, the long magazine profiles, the television specials. **Inside the Actors Studio with Adele Antoniades.** She had important things to say about craft, about honesty, about impulse, about precision. Sometimes the frustration of never being asked pierced Adele so painfully she felt she'd been burned inside. Run through with red-hot pokers. She'd had to stop watching television, mostly, for the vanity and the cowardice that poured from the screen. It disgusted her.

She could live here on the top floor, taking her little meals; they could send them up the inclinator. And she would sit on the deck and look out across the water far below. She'd have her hair swept into a topknot, for the airless heat—it was something about the position of the house, pushed there into the bush—and the mosquitoes would be ferocious, but she'd have coils, or zappers actually; the coils interfered with her breathing. She could do her yoga on the deck. And people would come for the weekend, they'd bring Aperol and French cheeses, and none of this was true because in two weeks the place would be on the market, and Gail had said, **Take anything you want,** but she didn't mean the house.

Adele rolled over and found her phone.

She checked her bank balance again, even though she knew nothing would have changed.

Nothing had changed.

She checked her emails to see if there were any from Lorraine, but there was no new message, just the summer-holidays autoreply.

She would tell Jude and Wendy about Liz. But later: after Christmas, sometime, never.

On the train she had heard Sylvie's voice, strengthening her.

Sylvie came to her in dreams and sometimes very clearly into Adele's conscious mind, like today. Just her voice saying Adele's name or even some irrelevant, meaningless thing. Like "Aspirin." Or "Hurry up." At first Adele had been afraid, but now it was nice. You couldn't tell when it would happen. But she knew that Sylvie, wherever she was, cared about her.

And Jude was downstairs waiting, capable and orderly. And Wendy, too, and Wendy's wobbly old self would help to warm the rooms made cool by Jude's unyielding, critical mind.

And Adele would give them . . . what?

At times she felt on the edge of discovering something very important—about living, about the age beyond youth and love, about this great secret time of a person's life. But she had not uncovered it yet, though it seemed to flourish in her dream life, which was an underground river of rich, vibrant meaning, flowing beneath her days. She knew this now, that it was not just your brain resting but a whole life being lived. . . .

Liz used to nudge Adele in the night sometimes, to stop her from snoring. How odd that this—the snoring—had become just a small indignity, when once it had been so shocking, to know such a thing about herself. Snoring was for men and fat old women.

Most often when Adele was exposed, or shamed, she turned for courage to the moment every actor knew: the moment on the stage, entirely yours, waiting in the pitch-dark before the spotlight came, the most powerful privacy a person could have. The fear drained away and adrenaline replaced it, and you were ready on your mark, in the darkness. Mighty already, because you were invisible. You held the whole place in your breath, it was all possibility and withheld force, and it was sexual, the build—until you were entirely ready to unleash it, wield it, wreak it. In that moment of taut, pure potential, everything, everyone, was yours.

This, it seemed, was to be taken from her. There had been no stage work, no television—not even a dying matriarch in a hospital bed, not even a walk-on—in a year. Her disbelief at this bit and tore. It was a savage force inside her. It made her weep, here in Sylvie's house.

Jude saw Adele's handbag on the kitchen counter and listened. There was no sound of movement in the house, even from above. It would be like Adele to be lying down, asleep even, Goldilocks in her just-right bed. Jude turned back to the pantry, pulled out some tins of peaches that were so ancient the labels had desiccated, and let them drop into the bin.

She had already taken one huge black bag of rubbish down to the verge, braving the inclinator, reasoning that if it carried Wendy's and Finn's combined weights, it could certainly take her and a bag of kitchen rubbish. As she descended, she watched the sky, where now and then a patch of streaky cloud lay against the hot blue. She had settled the bag against the driveway's stone wall and left it there. That felt good: progress.

Now she felt toward the back of the shelf, pulled out another jar of almost-empty Vegemite from the cupboard. Vegemite lasted forever, didn't it? But there were three jars already. **Thump,** into the bin.

She didn't care about the bedroom in the slightest —she wasn't fussed by trivia like that—but still, a fleck of disdain formed itself: How had Adele not, in all these years, developed a shred of restraint, of self-discipline? It was how and why she was an actress, Jude supposed. They were all children—the men, too, as far as she could tell. She could see the appeal, when you were young, the liberation of it. But what did it mean when you were old? What were you left with, still a child at seventy-two?

Adele had had a cosseting mother, which was probably the cause of it. And Sylvie did, too, whereas Jude's and Wendy's mothers were majestically awful. It was one of the things they shared over the years, gleefully. **You think** that's **bad,** and then they'd turn, grinning, to Sylvie and Adele, who were genuinely horrified, who cried, **You poor things!** and who could not laugh at the emotional crimes they'd never known it was possible for a mother to commit. But they didn't know the strength you got from having an awful mother, Jude and Wendy confided to each other. It taught you to stand up for yourself, to get **on** with things.

She bent and peered in and saw that another dark shelf of the pantry was now pleasingly empty.

When Adele woke, she was very hot, and groggy. She got up and went outside, stepping across the deck boards. Down below she could hear Wendy's high, wheedling voice. **Bloody** hell, it was true: she had brought the dog. Adele leaned out to see Finn, the crazed doddering creature, standing stiffly in the hottest corner of the deck. Wendy stood there, too, squinting in the blinding sunlight. Why would they not move somewhere into the shade! At Chinese reeducation camps, they made people stand in the sun for hours and hours. Adele almost called out to say this, but something downcast in Wendy's stance stopped her. She stood there with her hands limp by her sides in her grubby white T-shirt and a drab brown wrap-around Indian skirt. Adele loved Wendy, but why must she dress like a witless old hippie? It was not dignified. It made her look mad. Why would she do nothing about her appearance? Adele was afraid for her, the way she exposed herself. Her wild gray hair, her overstretched T-shirts with their logos and activist slogans, their fraying, rippling collars drawing attention to the loose flap of flesh at her throat.

Today she wore brown leather thongs on her long feet. Adele had seen those thongs close up, the way the soles had cracked and taken on the heavy shape of Wendy's big, mannish feet. The blackened toe marks made Adele feel a bit sick in some unnamable way. How could Wendy not understand that at their age nothing was more important than looking at the very least as if you were sane? Sometimes she wanted to grasp Wendy by the shoulders and shout at her, **You are old! Nobody wants to see this!**

She knew that the others thought her trivial, and she knew that they were right and that in some way this frivolity had damaged her life. She had not tried to develop her intellect as they had. Even Jude, whose job in the restaurant had after all been really rather menial (Adele breathed out, imagining for a moment having the nerve to say such a thing—she would not, ever) and who for all these years was just a kept woman (another breath . . .), even Jude somehow understood complex things about the world. About international politics and art movements. And ancient history and the names of the smaller cities in places like Jordan or Norway. How did that happen, from being a glorified waitress and falling in love with a rich married customer forty years ago? And Wendy . . . well, that was her work, thinking.

Adele envied their logical minds, their cool reason. Resigning herself to this complete lack in her own character had been very painful. But at the same time, she knew she had different, lesser but still-valuable things to offer. She had intuition, she had humanity—and beauty. What was wrong with that, in such ugly times? What was wrong with wanting to take part in life gently, with civility and attractiveness? It enhanced the world, enriched it, to create even the smallest pocket of beauty. Why must women be like men anyway, competing, controlling, at **war** all the time?

Often—this was by far the worst thing about Wendy—you could even see the terrible unevenness at her bust. Wendy seemed truly not to notice how it frightened people as they tried not to look, as the understanding dawned on them that Wendy had only one breast. Sometimes, Adele thought, there was something prideful in her display of it, how it made you feel vain for liking your own breasts. It was an assault: deliberate and violent. Adele prayed Wendy would wear the prosthetic if they went swimming.

Finn stood in that strange way at the

corner of the deck, his face close to the railings but absolutely motionless, staring straight ahead. How old the wretched dog was now, scrawny despite his swollen belly and ragged of spirit. It had been some time ago that Wendy was advised he must soon be put down, but she couldn't bring herself to do it. Poor Wendy. Adele saw something vulnerable in her friend, standing there. A great weariness, something in the slope of her shoulders. Adele wanted to cheer her—but now Jude, too, appeared on the deck, and Wendy stiffened to attention.

She would save them from each other.

She leaned right over the railing and called out in a jolly voice, "Hello, girls!"

The two women's faces turned upward, to the sun, to Adele. At the same instant, they each lifted a hand to shade their eyes, in a motion Adele had seen hundreds, thousands of times through all the decades of their friendship. She remembered them from long ago, two girls alive with purpose and beauty. Her love for them was inexplicable. It was almost bodily. She was conscious of breaking a bad spell, releasing them all.

"Finally," said Jude.

"I see you've got yourself the best room," called Wendy.

"I'll come down," Adele called back from her stage. Her mood lifted. It would be all right; they needed her, Jude and Wendy. She would protect them from each other.

She slipped lightly down the stairs.

I've got a list," Jude said, a piece of paper in her hand. She and Wendy had already begun, she advised pointedly, so Adele could start with the top bedroom, "Seeing as you've gotten yourself settled in there."

Adele was about to protest—she didn't take it, they had **given** her the room!—but then kept quiet, because the top bedroom held only a wardrobe and the chest of drawers to be cleared, nothing too demanding.

Wendy was to clean out the laundry, which made sense, Jude said, because Finn could still see her from out on the deck, and that way he would hopefully not cause too much more bother. Wendy and Adele exchanged a glance. They did not dare make a face, but Jude wouldn't have noticed anyway, reading down her list.

She would stay in the kitchen, because, Jude said magnanimously, it was going to take longest. She looked around at her kingdom, hands on her hips. "Certainly it's the dirtiest."

She turned to distribute the folded black garbage bags from the countertop. Adele could feel Wendy resenting that Jude was giving them orders again, but she herself simply shrugged. When had it ever been any different?

"I haven't even unpacked my stuff yet," grumbled Wendy, moving to her cooler bag on the counter.

• • • •

Jude gave an almost-but-not-quite-inaudible sigh and made a show of stepping around to the other side of the counter as if Wendy were already causing trouble, taking up too much space.

This is Sylvie's house, not yours, Wendy wanted to snap. Jude had bossed her since she'd arrived, dragging her out to the musty laundry before she'd even unpacked her things. She knew it was Finn. She'd angered Jude by bringing him, but everything angered Jude, whose distaste she felt radiating from across the room—about something as innocuous as groceries! She could feel it all the way from the other side of the orange countertop, where Jude was facing the dirty window, pretending to listen to Adele going on about Audrey Pierotti's sister losing an eye to melanoma.

"She has to get a false one **fitted,**" Adele said with relish.

But Wendy felt Jude's gaze coming backward through her shoulder blades, through the base of her skull, as Wendy drew from the cooler bag the packets and jars she'd tossed into it from her own fridge. At home it had felt freeing and spontaneous, not planning what to take, but now she saw that this was wrong. Under Jude's cold scrutiny, she saw how motley her collection was, how the very presence of her substandard groceries had somehow already marred the days ahead.

It was true that some of these things she should have left at home. She'd been in a hurry and hadn't had time for a list, but she could see it now. The ancient soy sauce could probably have stayed. Also the plastic bag with the few salad leaves, darkened and a little leaky at the bottom—she quickly thrust that back into the chiller bag. But here, here were also lovely things: some ham from the Italian deli and the good baba ghanoush—not from the supermarket but from the Sultan's Garden, where Jude had been and declared it a **terrific little place.** Wendy recalled that Jude had even particularly praised the baba ghanoush. And here now—the relief—was the unopened, obscenely expensive yogurt.

And half a pomegranate! The plastic wrap was a bit soggy, but once you sliced the blotched face away, there would be the fresh crimson jeweled beads, for those fancy salads everybody made now. Wendy herself had no idea what to do with pomegranate. Claire had left it in her fridge some weeks ago.

But here—ha! "Christmas cake! Homemade!"

Wendy held the silver-wrapped brick aloft in her two hands to show them. "Tessa Nassif made it for us. Well, for me. Here, let's have some, and a cup of tea."

"Oh, no," called Adele. "Jude's cake is much the best. Let's have that. Where is it?"

Wendy looked and saw that Jude was pleased.

Adele always knew how to flatter, but it was surprising to see Jude so taken in. Wendy turned away from them. **Fuck you both,** she thought savagely, and dropped the silver brick back into her bag from a height. She let it thud, accusing.

But instantly she was ashamed: "taken in" was one of her mother's bitter phrases. If you believed something nice another person said, you'd been taken in, had the wool pulled over your eyes. You'd been wrapped around their little finger, or they saw you coming. It had taken Lance a decade to train Wendy out of this nonsense and into love. She missed him again now, with the mighty heave of longing that still occasionally came galloping up from your gut, a force so strong and sad it might burst out through the flesh of your chest. If Lance were still here, it would be unthinkable to even notice such a silly remark, about **cake.**

She was appalled to find tears coming to her eyes, and she turned out of the kitchen door to check on Finn.

Adele made a face, but Jude simply moved across the room and took over the unpacking of Wendy's groceries. She properly unwrapped the oddments of food, wiped and sorted the jars, put clean plastic wrap on the pomegranate and a lump of cheese. Then she placed them carefully at the front of the refrigerator shelves to show Wendy that her contributions were acknowledged, were important. She took the stone of the cake, peeled back some sticky foil, and began cutting to serve some slices alongside her own, but once you saw it—pale and dry, horrid—it would only make matters worse, so she bundled it away again.

Wendy knew nothing about food at all. If someone told her this was their mother's recipe and the best cake ever, she believed it because it had been said. The evidence of her own eyes and mouth, her own senses of smell and taste and sight, when it came to food, had never interested her one little bit. It wasn't a criticism, it was just the truth. Nobody minded—Jude did not expect Wendy to care about food any more than Wendy wanted anyone else to quote her beloved Voltaire. It would be mystifying, a trespass, if such a transformation suddenly occurred. Why on earth was Wendy upset about it now?

The house was strange without Sylvie, that's why. Her absence cut them all adrift; this was why Wendy had been offended. Jude felt the bleak spasm of it behind her sternum. They were all lost. She must be kinder, Daniel had told her. She would talk to him later today, and he'd tell her again, and things would get better.

Adele, oblivious across the counter, had begun touching her toes, dipping and bobbing down to the mottled kitchen floorboards, then sweeping up again, arms wheeling gracefully. Her hands in a prayer position at her breasts, she asked, "Do you think you still need to blink, if you have a glass eye?"

When Wendy returned, Adele had gone, and from something in the way Jude stood at the counter, Wendy knew she had not meant to hurt her feelings about the cake.

They had always been able to understand each other, she and Jude.

But Adele **was** here. She swung up from the floor behind the counter and now swooped down again, ostentatiously pressing her palms to the floor, her famous breasts squished against her knees, her pert little bottom presented for all to see. Like a baboon. Really, she still did things like this. It was secretly impressive that Adele, so short and so bosomy, was yet so astonishingly flexible, able to bend herself into astounding positions that Wendy could never achieve even as a child. But the display of it all, this prancing about like some elderly sprite, was embarrassing. Wendy was tempted to say something.

"I've booked us a table at the bistro for dinner, by the way" came Adele's adenoidal, muffled voice, upside down from the vicinity of her knees. Wendy caught Jude's pained expression—then **whoosh!** Adele's flushed face appeared again, excitable and smiling, her upturned crests of high blond hair slowly collapsing.

"It's Locals' Night. It will be fun."

It would not be fun, but Adele would have her way. And now Jude and Wendy were mended, and it didn't matter about Tessa's cake, which was after all dry and quite horrible, Wendy knew that. Lance squeezed her shoulder and said into her ear, **See? Chin up, old girl.**

Adele saw the renewed ease between Jude and Wendy. She dropped her head and arms again, feeling the stretch in her thighs, painful and satisfying. She stayed down there, fighting the small loneliness that came upon her in moments like this. **They love you, too,** she reasoned, putting her flat palms to the floor. **They do.**

But love was not the same as respect.

CHAPTER FIVE

Jude plunged one glass jar after another into boiling soapy water, then set each of them, mouth down, on the draining board. She could stand the water very hot; decades of restaurant work had given her asbestos fingers. Finn appeared on the deck, transfixed by the trees. Or simply watching the air, stock-still. He stood to weary attention, staring. Why did the creature not sit, or lie down?

Jude sat down then herself, at the round breakfast table near the door; the hot water, it turned out, had made her a little light-headed. He couldn't have heard her move—he was **so** deaf now—but outside, mirroring her, Finn sat. And then swiveled in a strange, stiff rotation, using only his front paws, until he was directly opposite her, staring through the glass at her face. Could he even see her? She crossed her arms on the table and rested her head on them, keeping her gaze on his, but there was no flicker of recognition, even of movement, in his eyes. His tail lay flat and limp. There was nothing between them but a pane of glass, and she studied his face. The dark smudges of his clouded eyes brimmed with liquid, two mud pools in snow. His muzzle was grubby, too, the once-creamy fur stained and brown. His mouth hung open, black rubber lips slack, rippled. This was what happened to animals, and to humans: he was all failure and collapse, all decay. It was pitiful. Drool formed behind his long yellow teeth.

He shifted his weight, staring with a terrible patience at nothing through the glass, and then in his face Jude saw Sylvie's face appear, and from his mouth came Sylvie's sorrowful ghost breath, condensing on the glass.

She sat up straight in her chair.

"Finn! Finny!" Wendy's high voice came from the laundry along the deck, but the dog stayed, staring at Jude with Sylvie's reproachful, unhappy stare. There was a place between life and death, as between waking and sleep, and one day Jude, too, would know that place. This came to her, in Sylvie's steady animal gaze.

At last the dog lumbered to his feet, turned from Jude, and limped away.

The laundry was a small dank room behind the kitchen, entered only from the deck. It was Wendy's penance, to be deported here to the cobwebbed room.

She peered inside. There was the double

cement tub, the enormous and ancient top loader that shuffled noisily across the floor every time it was used, and a tall white linen cupboard whose doors did not shut properly. The chipboard swelled in little pustules, erupting here and there through the melamine.

Punishment was to be expected. But why did Jude not remember that Sylvie, whose house they were dismantling, was the one who actually **gave** Finn to Wendy? Sylvie wouldn't have banished him outdoors, she couldn't have cared less about things like a tiny bit of dog wee. Wendy knew that Jude's main concern would be keeping Finn away from her ridiculous sofa—which Sylvie had taken only because Jude was so insistent. You were not permitted to resist Jude's largesse. After she gave you something, she would badger you for months about its welfare. **How's the couch? Have you used that apple corer I gave you? Isn't it sharp!** IF YOU LOVE SOMETHING, SET IT FREE, stickers on cars used to say, but if Jude loved something, she held it captive even after she'd forced it upon you. **You know that scarf is silk—are you being careful when you wash it?**

Wendy felt better now that she had allowed herself this little blossom of spite. There was no point in saying any of these things, or even thinking them. It was just Jude being Jude.

The laundry door opened onto a narrow strip of decking that ran along the sandstone rock face behind the house. The angophora trees twisted and hung above. This outdoor corridor housed the drooping retractable clothesline and a rickety wooden wardrobe. Wendy flipped open its door to see sagging shelves of paint tins with dribbles down their sides and crooked lids, rusting cans of WD-40 and insect spray, paint rollers stuck to their trays, dusty cardboard boxes holding who knew what. She batted the door closed and hoped Jude would not notice the cupboard's existence. Let the new owners deal with it.

She called Finn, out of long habit—it

was only after she shouted, each time, that she remembered he could no longer hear her. She would have to fetch him, then settle him there in the shady corner beneath the clothesline where he could see her. Astonishingly, then, he appeared from around the corner. But once he sat, his tremor started again. She crouched beside him and stroked him and murmured, but there was something about the narrow space, or perhaps the dried eucalyptus leaves that shivered down the rock face in little drifts when the breeze blew, that was making him afraid. He stared about constantly, as if following the erratic flight path of an invisible fly, and licked his lips too much, pressed himself against Wendy's legs, trying to sit on her feet when she went to leave him.

Well, he could come into the laundry at least. She took a few steps and beckoned him, whispering. He limped after her, but at the open doorway he stopped, staring into the gloom.

What was going through his mind?

Wendy watched his innocent, fearful, dreaming eyes. He could not cross from the light into the dark alone.

She thought of Sylvie, the moment of death. Had she been afraid?

"I know, darling," she said to him, and she grasped his forelegs, dragging him into the space, his claws scraping, until he was safely across the threshold. Then he sank down on his arthritic hips and fell asleep.

She stood back and scanned the shelves in the cupboard and those above the tub. It was instantly clear that the laundry was an easy job: you just threw everything out. She pulled on some rubber gloves, took the garbage bag, made a nest of it on the floor, and began dropping things into it. Half-full boxes of laundry detergent set rock hard, cans of fly spray, stubs of burned candles, and cockroach-eaten matchboxes. The threadbare beach and bath towels she set aside—she could use those for Finn. But with everything else, on she went: plastic blister packs of screws, a broken gas lighter. A smoke alarm still in its packaging, so old that the label had faded to unreadability—she smiled; that was Sylvie. Into the bag all this went, along with a plastic basket of grimy vitamin jars, a bottle of shampoo. Why were these things even in here?

It was liberating, not having to think about the value of any of this stuff. There was a kind of black canvas wallet with a Velcro fastening so effective she couldn't rip it open. Something heavy was inside—who knew what? She let it fall into the bag.

Finn lay, his blackened snout resting along the cool concrete floor.

It was seventeen years ago that Sylvie had turned up at Wendy's house, a month after the funeral, with two cardboard boxes. It felt like last week, and a lifetime ago. The only other thing Wendy remembered about that time was the fact that every day for months and months she wore the same pair of Lance's old gray tracksuit pants and, when it got cold, his khaki gardening shirt over the top.

She found a stepladder, sturdy despite its

coating of cobweb and grime. She might take that home herself. From the top of it, she could see almost everything on the high shelf above the laundry tub. All of it was coated in black dust and mouse shit.

Sylvie had drawn out the small, white, bewildered puppy from one of her boxes. She did not try to make Wendy play with it, or want it. She'd put it on the floor and then emptied the other box: a bag of food, two bowls, a dog bed. It was a business-like distribution, as if Wendy had agreed to this, as if it were normal or generous to burden your grieving friend, who could barely dress herself, in this way. Wendy sat on the couch in numb disinterest—she had not the energy for anger at Sylvie, though it lay there, cold sludge in her gut.

Sylvie said, "Lab-poodle cross, if you can believe that. Designer mutt." Wendy said nothing. The ugly little dog waddled back and forth across her line of vision while Sylvie washed the dishes in the sink, put some soup to heat on the stove, changed Wendy's sheets, and put a load of laundry through the machine. She moved wordlessly through Wendy and Lance's house, sweeping and wiping and vacuuming. She hung the washing on the line. She set the table for two, pulled out a chair and pointed to it, and Wendy sat. They ate in silence while the small dog sniffed about their feet. As Sylvie left the house that day, she put a red leather leash into Wendy's hand and said, "In a fortnight you'll need to start walking him twice a day if you can, once at least."

And now Sylvie was gone.

Here was a plastic bottle of fabric softener with a label that could be from the 1980s. She let it drop; it made a cracking sound as it hit the concrete, not quite hitting the target of the bag.

Wendy's children had had their own grief to contend with. Jamie returned to London—or was it Stuttgart, back then?—within days of the funeral. And Claire, even then, was Claire. She told her mother to get counseling, left her a phone number for a psychotherapist, and went home to Bondi. People said, **It's good you have Claire,** but they knew nothing. Wendy was alone.

There was a stainless-steel fish kettle in here—one of those long, thin saucepan things to poach a trout in. **Covered** in dust. Wendy could not remember Sylvie ever once poaching a fish. She took the lid off, kept hold of the shelf with one hand, and with the other she dangled the pan, then dropped it in the direction of the garbage bag. She didn't want it to bounce and scare poor Finn, but this time she aimed right: it landed with a puffing sound, cushioned by plastic and rubbish. The lid joined it afterward with only a little noise.

The pan should not be thrown away, it was perfectly usable. It should at least go to the charity shop.

The baby Finn's life had burst outward, pulsated wildly in every direction, while she died in solidarity with Lance. It was a strange relief that her death mattered nothing to Finn back then. His little belly swelled alarmingly when he ate, and he slept on his back, legs fallen open. He had absolutely no idea of how vulnerable, how small he was. He was all body, all sensation, all greed. He barked at a pitch that pierced her brain. He wrecked everything—chewed her best shoes, tore tufts of kapok stuffing from the front of Lance's couch, ate half a manuscript and shat on the other half. He had to be walked, fed. He slowly returned her—most of her, the part that would ever be salvageable—to the living world. It was a cliché, and she loved him.

She was not sure if she had ever actually thanked Sylvie.

She sneezed.

But all this was in the past. And as a rule the past bored Wendy to death. Anyway, Sylvie knew; they were too close for thank-yous. Finn was Sylvie's as much as hers. So why must everyone obey the laws of Jude? She yanked irritably on a tangle of orange and yellow extension cords caught at the back of the shelf, sticky to the touch. And as the cords came down, so did a shower of mouse and cockroach shit and—too late to catch, although she tried and almost lost her balance—a heavy glass jug from a blender, which crashed off the edge of the cement tub and shattered into thick, curving shards on the floor. Wendy screeched; the jug's plastic base bounced near Finn's face, and he woke, terrified.

"Don't worry, don't worry!" she called to him—the glass pieces had shattered away from him, thank God—but it was too late, and off he went, hauling his barrel-chested frame upright, his body calling up the ritual before he was even awake, setting off on his exhausted, arthritic stagger, around and around in the tight, dark space.

He might walk in the glass! "Out of the way, Finny!" she cried, clambering down from the stepladder.

Once down, she grasped on to it for stability and leaned to pick up the glass. She felt slightly woozy—it was so airless in here. She had to sit for a moment on the middle step, her bottom squashed into the ladder frame, resting her hands on her thighs. She was sweating, panting a little. The smashing glass, the hurtling weight of the thing flying by her head, had given her a fright. Poor Finn was petrified, but he would be all right. She just needed to catch her breath. She felt the mouse dust entering her opened mouth.

Jude stepped out of the kitchen door and called along the veranda, "Everything all right?" There was no answer. It was exasperating, whatever had smashed—Wendy was so hopeless!

The tides of her feelings some days felt alarmingly chemical, hormonal, which of course was impossible: all that business was finished decades ago. She listened for Wendy to respond, standing on the deck, but she heard nothing except the electrical shirring of cicadas. She would have to go to the laundry and check. She started toward the back of the house but after a few steps found that she could not go on.

Sylvie's face had looked out at her from Finn's.

"Wendy? Are you all right?"

It was her own voice calling, but it came from her girlhood, from far away. She remembered the moment, aged thirteen, going under the anesthetic for her tonsils, slipping slipping slipping away, into a fizzling white nowhere. She gripped the wooden railing, which was hot beneath her hand.

Adele lay on her bed—**the** bed; she knew it wasn't hers—and surveyed the room, deciding where to start. There was the small pine dresser with its four drawers and the double built-in cupboards, very daunting. She supposed the dresser would be sold, and they could get some money for it. Gail could get some money for it.

She paused here for a moment of self-compassion, lying on her back with her elbows above her head. Here were Sylvie's friends working, clearing out Sylvie's house, and yet Gail would have all the benefit. Sitting there in Dublin waiting for the money to roll in. Sitting there in her Irish bog counting her sovereigns, or shillings, or whatever Irish money was.

But Gail was living in a glamorous new apartment with a view of the Liffey, and Irish money was euros, and there wasn't any bog, and it was racist, thinking things like that.

Jude was making ostentatious noises down in the kitchen, opening drawers and banging them shut, slamming cupboard doors. Getting things done, that was Jude. You had to admire her. Sort of.

When Adele told people about Jude's affair with Daniel, nobody could believe that neither she nor Wendy had ever met him, in forty years. But Jude wouldn't say his name to them, even now, and never had. It was as if she existed, always, on two planes at once: the one here with you and the other, her whole life lived with—without—Daniel. This was not difficult for Adele to understand. You had your ostensible life, going about the physical world, and then you had your other real, inner life—the realm of expression, where the important understandings, the real living, took place. Jude lived the life of an actress.

Now that she thought about it, she could not remember when they'd learned of Daniel's existence. Who had told them? Surely not Jude herself. It was bizarre that they could not speak to her about this, after forty years, but it was true. Adele and Wendy, however, discussed it with each other all the time; it never failed to interest them. Was Jude not lonely? Plainly, she was not. What kind of a feminist allowed herself to be kept in this way? Jude was dignified, appeared never to submit to anyone. Yet she had wasted her life on this man who must be kept secret, who gave his best self to his family and only what was left over to her, they said. But who could say what a wasted life looked like? Adele and Wendy had to fall silent on this, for Jude's affair had outlived both their marriages and two husbands' lives. And what of all their other friends? Susie O'Shane, and Stacy Milgate, Amanda van Heusen, with their buzz cuts and badges in the seventies, screaming **Dead men don't rape!** into megaphones, solidarity fists held aloft. Now Stacy had emphysema and was a drudge to her crippled, no-longer-philandering husband, and Mandy was permanently exhausted from grandmothering the teenage offspring of her princely barrister son.

And now, alongside Jude's affair, Adele's relationship with Liz—which had felt so real and solid—seemed insubstantial as a dream. She was washed anew with shame. She could not tell them, not yet. She couldn't say why, exactly, except that she would see the exasperation enter them, she would see the weariness in their eyes, the simmer of alarm that she would be asking them, again, for help. For money, for somewhere to stay. She would soon need to remind Wendy about the advance she'd already asked for. It made her feel ill, that she would have to ask, but Wendy—who had never wanted for money, it just flowed in from her work, from the famous book still on university lists around the globe, from her retirement fund, from Lance's clever investments—would already have forgotten.

A light suggestion floated dangerously before Adele: that she should—not legally, of course, but in a moral sense—be entitled to some kind of settlement, as Liz's de facto partner. But as soon as the thought formed itself, she knew it was despicable, and she hugged a pillow to her chest and had to squeeze her eyes tightly shut so as not to cry.

Something would happen, something would turn up. She heaved herself from the bed and opened all the cupboard doors, one, two, three. Take anything you want.

The cupboards were full—a wardrobe

with a few things drooping from luminous orange crocheted hangers, and then shelves above and below, crammed with things that made Adele feel tired and instantly bored. Dusty suitcases, backpacks with tangled straps. The handle of an umbrella stuck out, and there was a cracked lamp base (no shade), its dirty electrical cord dangling. There was a pile of French books and a stack of accompanying CDs. A checkered blanket, some vacuum-cleaner bags of the expensive kind. This was just the stuff she could take in at a glance. There was nothing to want here. Adele miserably began pulling the stuff out, onto the floor.

There was a crash from somewhere in the house below. Good, she thought. She wanted to smash something, too. Maybe she would. Maybe this heavy electric fan, which was the old style, made of metal, not plastic. But you could get money for something like that in a retro store in Newtown or Redfern. She held it for a moment, keeping her distance from its blades, which were thick with dust, and then carried it out onto the deck, where she stood at the edge, imagining hurling it over, letting it smash on the stairs, splintering the rotten wood into pieces. She put it down by the door and went back inside.

She pulled out a tangle of moldy-looking shoes—tennis shoes bent out of shape, one chewed-looking black rubber sandal with hideous rainbow canvas straps (that would be Gail's; Sylvie would never have gone in for that tatty hippie look), and a pair of quite good peep-toe camel-colored heels. But when Adele went to push her left foot into one, she felt an unnatural lump and then saw Sylvie's hard black orthotics inside. Orthotics made Adele revolted even to look at, with their lumps and ridges. She pinched her fingers to pick up the peep-toe shoes and flung them into a garbage bag. She glanced at her own lovely feet and felt lucky, then thought again of money and did not. She gathered the rest of the shoes and threw them into the bag, too.

Adele had learned many things about

herself from Liz over the past months. That she'd been guilty of a surprising moral pride, for example, about not having material things. When she had first taken Liz back to her studio flat (her **apartment;** nobody said "flat" anymore, Liz told her) and Liz saw Adele's meager possessions, she'd smiled and said, "You still live like a drama student." She meant the sarong covering the sofa, the Cézanne print on the wall. Adele was pleased, for this was something she had always been proud of: that she lived humbly, whatever her secret yearnings for wealth. But then she saw it wasn't meant as a compliment by Liz, who was a generation younger and had a diagnosis for everything, who called Adele a Second-Wave Feminist and saw her as quaintly naïve, and whose own spacious house was filled with deep couches and Wedgwood cups and five-hundred-thread-count sheets.

Until she met Liz, Adele had not known about thread counts. How could she not know? But she didn't. Once, not long before Liz invited her to come and live at Walker Street, she'd remarked kindly (was it kind?) that having broken furniture and chipped crockery didn't of itself make a person superior to others. And Adele quickly learned how delicious were five-hundred-thread-count sheets—this was one of the differences between a male lover and a woman, she discovered—and Riedel wineglasses and thick rugs made of pure wool, shot through with silk.

The idea of returning to the thin sarong on the couch and her little dark kitchen with its tiny window now frightened her. And without the Airbnb rent, how would the mortgage be paid? She returned to her mantra: something would happen, something would turn up, it always had before, it would again.

The clothes on the hangers were next. A pale blue cotton shirt with holes under the arms: out. She flung it, hanger and all, to the garbage bag, which was now a pile. A green raincoat that might do for someone, somewhere, but it was depressing. She was to be ruthless: she pulled it off the hanger, tossed it onto the pile. Here was another thing belonging to Gail: a floppy tie-dyed sort of arrangement—out—along with some other long dress thing, but oh, as she took the fabric of this one in her hands, she remembered it. It was Sylvie's pale turquoise dress, simple, chic. She held the hanger before her to look at it. It had a wide, scooped neckline and a loose square cut. Its drawstring waist gave it a sort of Grecian elegance. On the wrong body, it would look like a square sack with a tie around the waist, but on Sylvie it had been magical.

She turned to the mirror, holding the color against herself, and in the soft light it was beautiful. Adele was moved by the gift that had appeared here, just for her. She held the cool fabric to her face and breathed in Sylvie. For the first time, she thought about not having to drink Liz's kombucha anymore and not hearing

Milly's arch, opinionated young voice. The idea of abandoning the luxury that was never hers, which belonged to other people and which she knew in some obscure way was wrong, suddenly made her feel free and clean and young. She laid the dress down on the bed, then bundled up the French-language CDs and let them clatter, au revoir, into the garbage bag.

She had begun. Sylvie's room appeared new to her, fresh with possibility. Tomorrow was Christmas Eve. Great change was possible, Adele knew that. She felt it coming.

Wendy's heart banged too quickly. The air in the laundry was fuggy, causing this wooziness. Finn lurched in his circles in the moldy air, rocking and dipping as he moved, saving his painful front leg. He would go on like this for ages. The laundry felt very small, its shadows leaking malevolence.

She reached out with a foot and shuffled

the glass pieces together with the instep of her shoe, and then, with supreme effort and ignoring the pain in her shoulder, she lunged forward and snatched at the thick glass fragments, one-two-three-four, careful not to let their edges cut through the rubber gloves, and straightened, dropped them into the garbage bag. She was aware of her breathing.

She just needed some fresh air.

She peeled off the sweaty gloves and flicked them to the garbage bag; they missed, landing on the floor. No matter. She heaved herself to her feet, clutching at the bag's yellow plastic drawstring in the same movement. She dragged the bag behind her—it was surprisingly heavy now—until she was over the lip of the doorway and then stood on the deck panting, hands on her hips. The sky was still a hot, oily blue.

Finn glanced at her as he paced wearily on, around and around, trapped in the dim laundry and his unstoppable, mournful dream. "Oh, Finn," she whispered to herself, for she knew she could not reach him, that even his ability to recognize her was growing dimmer and dimmer.

And then—for no discernible reason—he emerged from his trance. He stopped circling and hobbled out of the shadows. He saw Wendy and slowly crossed the deck toward her, the dingy feather of his tail waving, and began to lick her leg.

Jude was relieved to hear the fridge opening behind her, and she turned—but it was only Adele, sighing about the heat and looking for ice to put in her grapefruit juice.

Wendy had still not emerged from the laundry.

What should she do with all the bags of stuff, Adele wanted to know.

"You're not finished already?" Jude said, trying to keep the stiffness out of her voice. She had done only two of the pantry shelves; surely Adele could not have sorted the entire wardrobe and the drawers in this short time. Adele looked in a dismayed way at the jars and bottles all over the counter.

"Aren't we just chucking everything out?"

Jude had been sorting through the bottles and packets, checking use-by dates, wiping the jars clean, ordering them into separate piles. Adele drank deeply and then added, a laugh in her voice, "I mean, we're none of us going to drag all this rubbish back home with us, are we?"

Jude was cornered, for she had planned to do exactly that with the things that were not yet past their use-by dates. The stock cubes and anchovies, tins of lentils that were perfectly edible, would be wasted if thrown out. She'd planned to share them among the three women. Adele's amusement was irritating.

Jude knew that Wendy could not be lying dead in the laundry, waiting to be discovered, though no sound had come again since the crash. She was too ashamed to ask Adele to go check, because she would have to explain why she had not gone herself. And of course it was ridiculous to panic in this way: Wendy was fine out there; she had just dropped something, in her clumsiness. More alarming was why Jude's own mind even went immediately to such melodrama.

More frightening than any of it was why she had seen Sylvie looking out of Finn's animal face.

Four months ago Jill Burton had slipped in her bathroom and lain on the wet tiles with a fractured spine for a day and a half before anyone suspected there was something wrong, and she nearly died in the hospital. She was still in the rehab place, would be for months.

Jude felt sweat around her hairline and turned to leave the room, to go see. How could she not?

But she couldn't. What would she say, coming around the corner to find Wendy perfectly all right? What would she do if there was something else, something dreadful?

Adele trailed away into the living room with her glass. Jude followed her, polishing a jar with a tea towel. She would somehow get Adele to go look.

"Let's go for a swim," said Adele.

Jude filled with fury: she wanted to shout that it was not a holiday not a holiday not a holiday, and what about Wendy's blood pooling over the laundry floor!

"Good God, it's so **hot**!" wheezed Wendy, clumping in from outside. Her face was terribly red.

Jude let out a long, funny breath. Wendy was not lying anywhere with a fatal head injury. She had not had a heart attack, she had not broken her back, but she looked very tired—and very grimy as she made her way toward the couch.

"Watch out for the sofa!" Jude screeched. She'd spoken more loudly than she meant to—the flood of relief had done it—and both Wendy and Adele looked at her coldly. But Wendy was covered in dust and dirt, and there was the pristine white sofa, and now Finn was beside her.

"Get him out!" Jude heard herself bellowing.

Wendy drew herself up, her woolly hair wild. "For **God's sake,** Jude. Can't you—"

Adele interrupted plainly, "Your leg's bleeding, Wend."

They all looked down at a long tear in the skin on Wendy's calf and the bright red blood that was curling down around her ankle.

Finn leaned in, licking helpfully.

It was a bit ghastly, holding Wendy's leg in her lap while Jude peered down, applying antiseptic and tape. An ancient first-aid kit lay open on the table.

"You should moisturize, Wendy," said Adele sadly. She was repelled by this close-up view of Wendy's powdery old skin, with its very fine few hairs, its blotches and moles. But she had to look at the leg, for she did not want to look at Wendy's feet in the leather thongs at this close range. She resolved to pay more attention to her own skin.

Wendy sat with her back straight and her big head up, calling to Finn outside the screen door. "Don't worry, darling, everything's all right." He was pacing again, of course. Adele and Jude had shooed him away from Wendy's cut leg with shouts and pushing, which Wendy blamed for making him anxious, and now he waddled slowly, exhausted, up and down the deck.

Adele thought of Finn's dirty tongue slurping at Wendy's cut leg. "I hope you don't get tapeworms," she said.

Wendy snapped that you got that only if your dog was infected and licked your face, and Finn was a **perfectly** healthy animal.

Adele and Jude looked at each other above the leg.

Wendy was shaken. She had cut herself on the broken jug pieces that tore through the garbage bag as she dragged it behind her, but she had not felt the glass glancing her skin. This, not the wound, was what had rattled her.

Adele understood. It was the specter hanging over them all. She had not ever mentioned her observations of Sylvie, at the time. The way she once dipped her hand into a cup of tea in the café, just quickly, once, twice, and then rubbed her hands together. It was so fast that Adele wasn't sure it had happened, and the others did not seem to notice. And anyway, what was wrong with that? What would she have said? There was another time—and soon afterward they got the news—when they'd been together at the theater, in the bathroom. Opening their cubicle doors at the same time, after flushing, she saw Sylvie lean down and dip her hand into the clean flushing water of the toilet bowl, draw it out, and flick the water from her fingers. Again, so fast it was almost unnoticeable. And afterward Sylvie had been so perfectly normal that Adele thought she must have imagined it.

And now Wendy had not felt a piece of glass slicing into her skin.

The secret trouble was that Wendy was simply old, in a way Adele—and even Jude—was not. Of course they were all the same age, or roughly, but even when they were young, Wendy had always seemed much older. Now, as she stared out at the dog, ignoring the fussing of her friends, Adele surveyed her face in a kind of wonder at the way its structure seemed to have collapsed.

When she was young, Wendy had been stunning in the powerful kind of way that frightened men—and women. It was strange to think of her now, that other, mighty young Wendy: the classics Ph.D. at Oxford, the youthful divorce and scandalous single motherhood before Lance, the internationally renowned books pounded out on the famously massive black typewriter featured in all the newspaper photographs of her. With her big glasses and her intellectual seriousness, smoking like Susan Sontag and writing her crushing commentaries, she would turn her great noble head to transfix you, or to wither you with a glance. Back then not caring how she looked made her sexy. There was also the fact of Lance's beauty, which was so devastating that it drew Wendy into its radiance and made her beautiful, too. That handsome, urbane Lance chose Wendy instead of someone to match his own looks and class gave him integrity and created an aura of strange attraction around her. People—interviewers, filmmakers—spoke of Wendy as having a powerful, blazing allure.

But now, sitting here in the kitchen with sticking plasters arrayed along the big tear on her freckly leg, she seemed to have shrunk, and the planes of her mighty cheekbones and jaw had tilted somehow, inward and down, so that to Adele it seemed she'd begun, impossibly but surely, to look really very much like Norman Mailer.

• • • •

Wendy lay in her bedroom, where she'd been sent to rest. Part of her was insulted at the way Jude and Adele had patted her and ministered (and the nasty way they'd shouted at Finn!), giving her orders and at the same time being unusually—suspiciously—tender. But another part of her was glad, for she needed uninterrupted space to think about her work. Out on the deck, after smashing the jug, she'd had some realizations, and she must consider them before they vanished.

Adele had let her sneak Finn into the bedroom from the veranda, and he, too, rested now, flopped down on the brown-and-white velour dog bed. He watched her from his stripy nest, and she watched him. She would be able to tell from the look of anxiety on his face if he was about to piss; if she kept an eye on him, she could scurry him outside in time.

What had occurred to Wendy as she sat outside the laundry, breathless in the humidity and the cicada noise, a little jolted from the smashed glass, was that there were . . . **energies**—wrong word, a crude approximation, but it would do for now—surging all around her. The angophora trunks curved and undulated, moving, gesturing. The earth was giving out messages. The energies were in the air itself, in the shock of the crash, in the colliding gusts of furnace-hot wind and the shady light—and these rhythms, these messages, were connected somehow to the central plank of her argument. She could skew the introductory chapter in this direction. It could—could it?—frame the whole thing.

It was nice to lie down, she had to concede. Her leg, propped on a set of pillows by Adele, throbbed pleasantly.

She felt a flicker of alarm that she was suddenly unsure how to spell "ache." She went through it in her mind, putting down the letters, which surely were correct. But there looked to be something missing. If she were typing, it would come out right, body memory would make sure. Her fingers did the work of her mind. But this sort of thing had begun to bother her. She noticed herself spelling things wrong, very simple words. She sometimes typed "shit" instead of "this."

The pissant's words from three years ago returned, treacherously. **Wendy Steegmuller has now reached her seventies. For a public intellectual, this is a dangerous time.**

She remembered the morning she read it, on the way into her building at the university. She had stopped reading, lowered the paper, stared, unseeing, at the gentle Tongan cleaner, Marshall, steering his mop over the tessellated tiles of the Moorehead portico.

As a long-term admirer, I can imagine no reviewer wanting more success for this book than I. However.

She had seen the pissant once after this, bellowing over the counter at the bookshop. "**Strategikon** of Maurice!" he'd shouted, oblivious to the loudness of his voice, his ridiculous flowing hair. The young man behind the counter looked blank, typed on his keyboard, shook his head sorrowfully. As if stating the obvious, the pissant added, "It's a Byzantine military **handbook**!"

Of course they didn't have it; nobody did. Wendy had relished her unspoken exchange with the mystified young man, their shared raised eyebrows and ironic smiles after the pissant had gone. And she'd enjoyed even more knowing that **she** had a copy of the **Strategikon,** safe at home in Lance's study. Never to be lent.

Here in the bed she was overcome by a great tiredness. At times the effort required to propel her own body through space surprised and demoralized her. On days like this, she felt as if her body were a waterlogged eiderdown she must drag along behind her; she longed to shrug it off, to spring forward without effort into the hours ahead. Her mind required lightness, quickness, if a working day were to proceed well. She could not be hampered by the insolent inadequacies of the body.

Her leg really did ache.

She reached for her notepad, and as she

did, a vision appeared: the book would be a mosaic—not linear, yet not without order. A sort of mandala! She would show the pissant. Radical, a complete departure from what she had done before—that was the way for her now. Excitement rippled through her. Voltaire worked until the very end. And what about Churchill? And in Picasso's last four years, he had painted in a frenzy, more than in any other four years of his life. Wendy had **decades** to go.

She could feel it starting, the fizzle of important discovery—if only she were home in her office instead of here, if only it were not so damned hot—but the good simmering was here, the discordance of fresh provocation, harmonic and surprising, beautifully cadenced like Yo-Yo Ma in her ears, and here was Wendy Steegmuller, with the same undimmed intelligence that had shaped the only important conversations in this country (and beyond! **The Subterranean Kingdom** had been received rapturously in New York and San Francisco, in Boston, in Paris and Oxford!)

for six decades, and she would not be stopped just because she'd been cut and didn't feel it, or because the pissant's pathetic little barbs came to her sometimes in the night, or because her middle-aged daughter found some dried cheese on a grater in a drawer.

A fresh wave of bitterness came to her about Claire.

It was quite difficult, at times, to stop herself from remarking on the banal concerns that appeared to rule Claire's life. Could this really be her own daughter, with her teeny books about magical tidying-up, her environmental cleaning mittens, her prissy gold jewelry? Where had Claire learned to be so petty? Once a university medalist, and now look at her, blithering about cookbooks and **bakeware,** captive to that degraded capitalist language, rummaging in her tight-lipped way through Wendy's utensil drawers in search of something to shame her with. Wendy knew that Claire thought her own silence about the grater was embarrassment. She would never apprehend that all her mother felt toward her in that moment was pity.

Finn raised his head, challenged Wendy. All right, then: not just pity, anger, too. How could she? After everything I. The words Wendy never spoke.

It was true Wendy was further along the timeline of her life than she might prefer. This was obvious, and yet more and more she found, in place of urgency, a kind of spongy spaciousness, commanding her to slow down. Occasionally this feeling was so great, swelling up inside her, that she failed to work at all. Where was the whirring guilt, running along beneath everything she did that was unrelated to work? Where was the vigilance, inspecting herself for laziness, the compulsion for achievement pushing her onward through her own resistance?

There was no logic to this. She had labored in such frenzies at twenty and thirty, when time stretched out in great oceans before her.

If she wanted to, she could return to

that time in her mind. After her first—inconsequential—marriage, before Lance, when Claire was a baby. She could marvel at how she had worked through the exhaustion of single motherhood, in that grotty little Redfern terrace. Going down with the baby when she put her to bed at seven, waking with the alarm at eleven, working at the kitchen table till four in the morning before snatching another two hours of sleep. How had she paid the rent? Transcribing? Odd that she could not remember—but it bored her, to look back. The future was what mattered.

She had no regrets. How astonished she'd been after the second birth, with Lance to help her—it was so easy with two of you! Lance doing feeds, Lance gathering morose little Claire, staring silently from room corners, into his arms and loving her like his own child.

And the children had thrived despite the grot, whatever Claire thought. No matter what happened later with Jamie, in that mysterious, fleeting period. The children were part of the work, and the work was part of her being their mother; that was the point of everything she did, the inseparability of women's intellectual and emotional and bodily labor. You could see it as a burden or a blessing, but the aim was integration, not conquest.

Wendy doubted that Claire or Jamie had ever read either of those early books, written over their wriggling, shrieking, sleeping, weeping, vomiting little bodies. It was astonishing now to think of how her own body had endured. What a sturdy, reliable workhorse it had been. She felt pride for it, this beloved lost child, her own strong body of the past. And pride, too, for her mind of that time: forceful, original, persuasive. But—this was interesting now—there had been hysteria, too. The early works that had made her name now seemed to her fervid, attention seeking. Her intellect had only deepened with the years, which was a relief. And it was why this new one would be something. It was urgent—and yet she must proceed languidly, without grasping. Happiness spread through her, that her instincts were still sure.

But Claire, her own flesh, saw none of it. All that Claire saw, whenever she came into Wendy's orbit—so infrequently, so resentfully—was deficiency. Wendy looked down at the dressing on her outstretched leg. This limb looked strange, as if it belonged to someone else, a swollen old foot turned outward at the end of it.

Claire entered her house without knocking and strode about snatching up coffee cups and newspapers, dispatching them with professional efficiency into the dishwasher, the recycling bin. She inspected Wendy's fridge, her dishes, her laundry basket, even. Worst, the very worst, was how she would sniff the air in Wendy's house and shrivel her nostrils, then pretend she hadn't done it. Afterward she'd stomp around opening windows.

How dare you? Wendy wanted to snarl.

Two days ago Claire had stood looking down at Finn in an appraising, clinical way, and declared, "It's time to put him down, Mum. He's a mess, he doesn't have a clue what's going on. He doesn't even know you're here."

An outrage. Wendy responded calmly that of course he did, and she called him, but poor Finn could not respond, paralyzed by the icy gaze of Claire. Wendy called him again and then willed him silently, **Come on, darling,** but Finn stood with his face to the wall. And then began turning in his circles. All this tension had made him anxious, but that couldn't be explained to Claire, who turned her triumphant, faux-sorrowful smile on her mother.

"Mum"—her voice soft then, treacherous—"he's shitting everywhere; he can hardly walk. He's oblivious and frightened. You're only keeping him alive for yourself. It's cruel." And as she turned to pick up her enormous stiff leather handbag, she swept her slow, insulting gaze around Wendy's house, lingering on the cobwebs, the chipped skirting boards, the plate with its hardened egg yolk, the dog beds and towels, another pile of papers that curled at the edges.

"You have to start making some decisions, Mum," she said. A parking officer issuing a warning. And she moved off down the dark hallway of Wendy's house without saying good-bye.

Claire could go to hell. And so could Jamie, who never even bothered to get in touch, or hardly ever. Wendy surprised herself with the viciousness of these feelings toward her own children. She loved them, had devoted her youth, her life, to them! But now it was a matter of survival.

She shifted on the pillows and exhaled a long, slow breath, emptying her mind of Claire's patronizing voice and the unspoken trailing end of her sentence—**before someone else has to make them for you.** Emptying her mind of both of them, their ridiculous resentments. What had she not done for them? She emptied out Jamie's snarky little jokes about her leaving all her money to the dog. All what money? What an insult.

She closed her eyes and returned to the possibility she had felt out on the deck, the swelling and blooming of ideas. It was too early for a theory, or a cohesive metaphor, even, about the rhythm surges. But she knew the glint of fire in it. There was work to be done, and radical exploration. She was the explorer. She had made her decision, and it was **work.**

Finn lifted his head and yawned sweetly at her. She heard his jaw click. It was not time to be put down. They would prevail.

CHAPTER SIX

The beach was only twenty minutes' walk from the house, but Jude and Wendy both flatly refused. "I'm not trudging up that hill in thirty-one degrees," Jude said firmly. Wendy had merely pointed to her leg.

But it would be good **for you,** Adele wanted to plead. **Both of you,** imagining Jude's splintery, desiccating bones, Wendy's breathlessness. **If you only walked more hills,** she wanted to say.

"We'll drive," said Jude, ending the matter.

Wendy said to wait while she fetched Finn's lead.

"Just leave him here, tie him up!" said Adele. "He won't remember anyway."

"I can't, he'll howl," said Wendy. "And then he'll never settle later. He gets much worse when he's stressed."

"Oh, for God's sake," said Jude.

Wendy turned to her peevishly. "That's the twentieth time you've said that today."

They all looked through the glass at the dog, who stood on the deck, head and chest partially hidden beneath the outdoor table. After a brief snooze on the towels, he had returned to staring duty and stood there, motionless, for another half hour.

It could send you mad, looking at him. Adele remembered film footage of catatonic schizophrenics, sitting in their sludge-gray clothes, completely still and spiritless. Yet they could catch a ball. If you threw an orange at Finn, it would just thud from his body to the ground and roll away.

"It's not his fault, he's in a strange place." Wendy looked hurt, as if she had heard Adele thinking. There was a silence while nobody asked, **Well, whose fault is that?**

When they reached the street—Jude making her way cautiously down the stairs behind Adele, trying but failing to copy Adele's confident descent while Wendy and Finn rode the inclinator, the dog pawing and whining—Wendy began to lead them to her car.

"Finn can go in the back," she said. "It's all right," she added testily, seeing their hesitation, **"I cleaned it out."**

Another look passed between Adele and Jude.

"Well . . ." said Adele. It would be only a few minutes.

But Jude would not buckle. "Look, Wendy," she said crisply, "I'm sorry, but you're a terrible driver. It's too frightening. We'll meet you there."

Wendy stood with her mouth open. Finn had slid down and now lay at her feet, face on his front paws. After all the standing and pacing of the morning, he now looked as if he might already be asleep.

What Jude said was true and had been for at least a decade. Whenever Wendy drove, she chattered nonstop, glancing constantly about instead of watching the road. She appeared to have almost no concentration and zero forethought, swerving wildly at the last possible moment to change lanes. Her foot fell on and lifted from the accelerator completely at random, surging forward, faltering and jerking without warning or reason. Usually they made excuses about the state of Wendy's car, filthy and filled with the detritus of her life—plastic bags, dog beds and hair-covered towels and blankets, textbooks, university parking tickets, rotting apples. As often as possible, Adele arranged their meetings in the city, at places with impossible parking, ensuring that they'd all need to take a train or a taxi.

Wendy stared at the two women, incredulous. "I've never even had an accident!" she protested. She yanked on the leash, dragging Finn awake, pulling him toward the Honda and opening the passenger door.

But Jude was already standing by her glossy black car.

"Sorry, Wend," said Adele tenderly.

It was too late for kindness. Wendy ignored Adele and instead bent stiffly to gather the dog, hauling him into her arms with a little grunt. She kicked the passenger door open wider and lowered him to the seat, then slammed the door shut before stalking around to the driver's side. She didn't look at them again. Were her eyes red? It was difficult to tell if she was crying.

Jude maneuvered herself into her own hot car and bent forward to change her shoes. From the passenger seat, Adele caught sight of Jude's bare feet—pale white, pushed out of shape with bunions, with hard little gray stubs for toenails. This glimpse made Jude seem suddenly, unthinkably vulnerable.

Adele put her hand to the air-conditioning vent, and cool air began to pour over them immediately. Jude's car—who knew what it was, except expensive—really was very lovely, its taupe leather seats cool beneath your back.

There was a time they were quite sure Jude had anorexia. Many years ago, back when she was still running the restaurants, she grew thinner and thinner. Adele heard rumors from theater people who spent late nights in the brasserie that Jude was a heroin addict, which Adele knew was ridiculous. But there was definitely something wrong. Jude chattered with a strange brightness, always with a vodka tonic in her hand, and she kept her arms and chest covered even on the hottest days, wore voluminous silk scarves around her neck. Adele convinced Sylvie to confront her about it, and Sylvie came back very upset and said she didn't know, but that Jude had sent her packing. Sylvie and Jude didn't speak for a year or two after that. But at a certain point, Jude seemed to get better, seemed to emerge from her brittle trance; her body did not feel so insubstantial when you kissed her hello, and slowly Sylvie and Gail were allowed back into her circle.

Was all this before or after she met Daniel? Adele had not thought about it in decades.

Now Jude reversed out of the driveway, the vehicle gliding in a single smooth, protected movement. The car felt wadded with a thick, insulating layer of money, its engine softly humming as it eased onto the road.

"Oh, God, there she is," Jude murmured into the rearview mirror as they swept along the road to the beach. "Don't look," she instructed, and Adele, who had begun to turn around, obeyed.

But once in the beach car park, they waited for Wendy, who had trailed behind—they'd lost her along the way. Maybe she would not come, maybe she'd driven off somewhere else instead.

"You didn't need to be so brutal," said Adele.

But Jude only sniffed, "It's time she was told. She might be more careful," and returned her gaze to the ocean, vast and blue.

Adele watched Jude standing there, tall and straight-backed, a chic older woman at the beach. She wore an oversize, very fine straw hat and big black sunglasses, the hems of her black linen pants loosely rolled, and a white muslin shirt trailing flatteringly past her slim hips. Even her feet no longer looked sad, but elegant in her black Birkenstocks. The frailty Adele had seen in the car was gone; Jude was back in command.

Be careful, Adele wanted to say. It was dangerous business, truth telling.

"Oh, come on," said Jude, gesturing to the beach. "She'll find us."

• • • •

Adele was so relaxed about her body, Jude thought. Another person might not say relaxed, might instead say deluded. She was leading the way now over the sand, striding through all the couples and families, unfazed by the kids swerving around her to charge into the waves with their boogie boards. Adele wore only her swimsuit and a sarong tied tightly at her hips, the cloth flapping open now and then to reveal the fake tan on her short, freckled legs. Her breasts sat low in the swimsuit, its plunging red neckline showing too much crepey décolletage, her flesh spilling over the sarong, over the straps, which cut into her pudgy back.

The word Jude's mother would use for the way Adele dressed was "trashy." It was the word she did use, in fact, even though Marlene loved Adele, and Adele showed her more kindness than Jude could ever manage. Each time Adele left her after a visit to the nursing home—after Marlene kissed her with her old, dry lips, calling her **darling,** obsequiously thanking her—she'd wait only until Adele had left her line of vision before smirking and saying, "She really thinks she can still get away with that, doesn't she?" Jude was sure Adele must have heard Marlene's barbed remarks, many times. But she never said anything about Marlene that wasn't a compliment. Somehow Adele had an unending well of kindness for people whom Jude found intolerable. She quietly marveled at this capacity in Adele, in the way you could admire someone's proficiency with an expertise that you yourself had no interest in mastering. Like knitting, or salsa dancing. Wendy once asked Jude if it hurt to see Marlene behaving so sweetly toward Adele when she was so vile to Jude herself. The question surprised her. All she felt when Marlene switched her gaze away from her to beam at Adele was relief.

Now she found she had to take off her sandals on the sand, and her hat kept lifting, threatening to blow off. Despite the breeze it was still unbearably hot, too humid for this trekking along the sand.

She willed Adele to stop walking now and sit down on the shore. They shouldn't go too far anyway—they needed to make sure Wendy could reach them.

She twisted around to see Wendy finally lumbering along the beach far behind them. She was dragging the poor crippled dog, who used his frail remaining strength to strain sideways on the leash, afraid each time of the little slapping waves' white foam sliding toward him. It would be kinder to let him range farther from the water, but the leash was too short, and Wendy stayed resolutely on the hard wet sand. It was her hip, Jude knew, that meant she couldn't tolerate the unevenness of the soft sand, and even on the flat she rocked from side to side, her big, loose body swaying.

Jude shrugged off the memory of Marlene staring up at her, parked there in the ugly musk-pink vinyl of the recliner (**why** were nursing homes and hospitals always decked out in these revolting colors?). By the end, when Jude wheeled her to the dining room, Marlene would simply dab at the table, her hands pinched into claws. By that time she no longer knew what food was for, could not recognize Jude. No longer knew what a daughter was, or a spoon, but the cruel body pressed on, enduring. Sometimes she lowered her wavering tortoise's head and croaked out shockingly lucid insults. She once said, "You still sniffing round that old Jew?" and chewed something nonexistent in her mouth, staring at Jude's bony chest. Jude had gotten up and left the room and had not gone back for a month. But for the final year of her mother's life, she visited the nursing home once a week out of self-pity and pride and duty. Marlene had finally died at ninety-nine and four months of age in August, at last settling Jude's deepest, most unspeakable dread: that she would not outlive her mother.

Jude hated the elderly. She always had, even as a child, when other children adored their grandparents, flinging themselves at their soft, unsteady bodies. All her life the elderly had disgusted her; it was their patchy skin, their need, their capacity to see things in you. The decay inside their secret old mouths. She would never become one of them. She had an advanced-care directive. She had kept a note of the website that would sell you Nembutal. She had Daniel.

She knew there was something wrong with her, she knew this disgust meant something psychological. She was old herself now. She knew that.

When Wendy finally looked up, after getting herself and Finn from the car park to the sand, untangling his forelegs from the lead, she saw the bright white curve of the beach, the shocking blue water—and she saw Jude and Adele far ahead, heading off down the beach without her.

So this was how it would be, these days at the house, with no Sylvie and the distance stretching and deepening between them all. She stood watching the expanse opening up. Even the two of them weren't walking together. Until now she had never considered that the worn rubber band of their friendship might one day simply disintegrate. It seemed impossible. But a deadness had crept into their feelings for one another and, it seemed now, was spreading. She thought of the Barrier Reef, and coral bleaching, and it made her want to cry: the ugliness, the devastation of all this loss.

She watched their little procession down the beach. From a distance the contrast between the two women was even more striking: Adele's prideful stepping out, separating herself from the shrouded, buttoned-up Jude, who leaned into the soft breeze as though it were a tornado, clutching her ridiculous oversize hat. Jude's mouth, Wendy knew, would be set in its customary grim line, the expression that meant she would endure without complaint but she would not enjoy. Wendy knew that expression so well it was as familiar as her own face.

She straightened. It was all right. In two days she would be home with her work, and in this moment Finn was here, and he needed her. "Come on, Finny," she crooned, and tugged on the leash, and at last he seemed to register her presence again and began to move.

Thankfully, Adele slowed down and finally stopped. By the time Jude reached her side, she was making a show of taking off her sarong and laying it on the sand, then flopping down on her back. She rested on her elbows, knees up, arching her spine and tipping back her head with closed eyes, offering herself to the golden afternoon sun. As she neared her, Jude looked around to see who else was embarrassed, amused, by this posturing. But in all the families and couples and groups of teenagers on the beach, it seemed none had even noticed two old women on the sand.

She set down her beach bag, careful to

breathe evenly and quietly despite feeling so puffed, and flicked out a black-and-white towel. She lowered herself, making sure not to emit any effortful sounds; Adele was already smug enough about her flexibility, the strength of her healthy body. Jude sat resting and looked out at the sea. Then she turned to see Wendy laboring along, her hair flailing beneath some sort of baseball cap, tie-dyed pants flapping, hauling Finn behind her.

The dog was just a dog, a poor animal kept alive for too long. There was nothing mysterious or ghostly about his pathetic aged body, lurching painfully along the sand. Jude turned back to the sea, and something settled in her, soothed by the flop and drag of the waves.

Eventually Wendy made it to Jude's side, panting herself, her face sweating. But instead of sitting down on the sand, she began to command Finn. Jude watched her saying **Sit,** calmly, over and over. Bending to the dog, making eye contact, speaking more loudly, trying to get him to hear. “Sit, Finn,” sternly. Again and again. It was futile, anyone could see that, but still Wendy persisted, her voice patient and loving. Finn did not sit, only stared at the ocean with his mouth dropped open, breathing fast and shallow. Then he started a high, nervous whine, turning his dog head to Jude, and Sylvie’s watery eyes pleaded with her again.

Jude stared back, appalled. Quickly she faced the sea, hugging her knees tight.

Her heart jolted in her chest. What could this mean? She was going mad.

Once, about sixteen years ago, she’d thought she was having—knew, in fact, that she did have—a stroke. The moment was crystal clear in her memory: cocooned in a deep green velvet sofa at Donovan’s in London, listening to Daniel, she felt it happen. She felt a line being drawn slowly along the inside of her skull. A thread pulled taut from temple to temple, drawn slowly backward over her brain, to the base of her skull. A peeling sensation. Not painful, not even unpleasant. But in that moment she felt time and distance stretch between her and Daniel, and she knew she could not reach him, could not speak across it. A moment later it was as though nothing had happened. She didn't mention it; they went to bed. The next morning she looked closely at her face in the mirror and thought she could see the slightest lowering of eyelid, mouth, on the left side.

It was a long time ago. She had never told this to anyone.

She exhaled a slow, complete breath now and made herself turn again to look at Finn. Sylvie was gone. The dog stared back at her with his clouded, uncomprehending eyes.

Her heartbeat slowed, and she felt the blood drain out of her. Anger replaced it. It was detestable that Wendy should drag the poor creature everywhere with her like some kind of rotting security blanket. It was cruel and pointless. But Wendy went on and on, uselessly calling him to attention.

"Sit down, Wendy, for God's sake," Jude snapped.

Jude wished again that Sylvie, real Sylvie, were here. Only she could have convinced Wendy to leave Finn back at home—with Claire or in a kennel. Only Sylvie, whom Wendy had always slavishly idolized and obeyed, would be able to convince her to put the damn dog to sleep. And Sylvie would have made this a pleasant, easeful trip to the beach instead of a battle of wills.

But if Sylvie were alive, this trip to the beach would not be needed. She would be in South Australia with Gail, they would each be having ordinary Christmases, and there would be no grieving contest among these three strangers. These three—four—failing, struggling creatures on the sand.

Wendy's hip was painful, but Finn was calmer now that they sat in the soft dry sand, away from the alarming slap of the waves. She took off her cap and lifted her hair from her neck. It was good, despite the heat, to be in the fresh, briny air with the crystalline sea before them. Finn was lying down now, breathing softly, his head on his paws. The bony furrows of the sand pushed therapeutically at her buttock, soothing her painful side. She brushed sand away from the Band-Aid on her leg.

Something in the wide blue ocean could transform you, if you surrendered to it.

But here beside her were her two friends, their same scratchy old ways. Adele's vanity, Jude's disdain. She didn't care any longer about the driving business (Jude had revealed herself there, showed her special brand of controlling hysteria). She preferred her independence anyway. But she wondered again, sitting on the shore beside them: Why did they still come together, these three?

The gulls circled overhead, screeching. Finn snored lightly. Animals were simply themselves, obeying instinct. It was only Wendy who knew that they were animals, too, she and Jude and Adele.

They came because of duty. Because of Sylvie, and for Gail. Because they always would. Because what was friendship after forty years? What would it be after fifty? Or sixty? It was a mystery. It was immutable, a force as deep and inevitable as the vibration of the ocean coming to her through the sand.

Wasn't it? She didn't know.

The sun was beginning to lower itself behind them, and soon it would sink below the ridge of land across from the beach. It was turning the sand a supreme gold. Across the sea, near the far horizon, a bank of cloud gathered. This was the last of the day's sunshine, and it made the deep, pure blue stretched out before them more precious, more inviting.

Finn turned his head, still asleep, but his muzzle twitched. Wendy watched his closed eyes. Did he dream, still? Did he recognize smell any longer? Who could tell? She ran a soft hand over his swelling belly, rising and falling there on the sand.

"I'm going in." Adele was standing, tugging and flicking at her red swimsuit beneath her bottom cheeks, marching into the water. The suit looked expensive, upholstered and paneled, sucking and lifting her flesh into acceptable form. Adele's commitment to her body was a source of everlasting fascination to Wendy. Who could be bothered, now? But she did look marvelous, striding over the sand in her taut red swimsuit, blond hair piled high, moving without shame as though she were thirty, twenty, sixteen. As though she could wield her body's power, possess the water with it like any ageless girl.

Beside her Jude, too, watched. Wendy could feel the envy coming off her in waves. For a moment it was possible to feel sorry for Jude.

"You going to swim?" Wendy asked quietly. She waited for an olive branch from Jude.

Jude lifted her chin at the water, hugged her knees. "Not yet." She did not look at Wendy, but she held out her hand for the dog's leash. That was as close to an apology as she would offer. Wendy gratefully dropped it into her hand and began unpeeling her clothes.

In her peripheral vision, Jude saw Wendy, still seated, struggling out of her T-shirt, her pants. Finn woke and stiffened, watching anxiously for her face to reappear from beneath the fabric of the shirt. Then Wendy let out a low groan of effort as she clambered awkwardly to her feet and stood facing the ocean in a threadbare navy one-piece. The sticking plasters made a line along her shin, but there was no blood. Wendy said to the air, "Don't worry, I'm not going to **offend** anybody," waggling the pale jelly blob of an aged prosthesis by her side for Jude to see, then slapping it expertly into her swimsuit in a motion so practiced she didn't even look down while she did it.

She waddled stiffly down to the water then, the flesh of her body loose inside the sagging fabric of the suit. Jude could see Adele peering at Wendy across the water, inspecting for the prosthetic. Strange, how even without your glasses you could see your friend in the distant water and know from the tilt of her face what she was thinking. And strange how you could still be so very alone.

Jude could not tell Wendy she had **never** been affronted by her missing breast. The very thought was an affront, that she would feel anything but pride for Wendy's survival. It should go without saying that Jude had never seen anyone as brave as Wendy when her life was threatened, when she lay sweating in chemo fevers, so nauseated she could not eat, nor even drink water some days. Lance changing her sheets in the middle of the night, Lance shopping and cooking and cleaning in the way he always had, but so tired himself he hardly had the strength to thank the rest of them for their small offerings of food, of driving Wendy to chemo, and still he did thank them. Jude was awestruck by that majestic, exhausted, monumental love. And still was moved, each rare time she noticed Wendy's flat side. That scar across her heart so old now, that terrible time so absolutely obliterated by the nobility, the courage of Wendy.

Wendy must have noticed how Jude pounced (every time!) on Adele's silliness about the prosthetic. It would sound bizarre, hysterical, to say these things about Wendy's character aloud. But Wendy must surely know she felt them.

Jude watched them. Adele was appeased, there in the water. She raised an arm to beckon Wendy in, and then Wendy's squeal at the chill water's grip could be heard over the waves and the gulls. When the water reached her thighs, she ducked below a wave and stood, hooting, and then slowly breaststroked her way to Adele. Soon the two women lay and drifted and lounged in the water, chattering like girls.

• • • •

In the ocean Adele felt it with her whole body. **I am reborn.** She tumbled in the water, spun, luxuriated. When she came up, she saw Wendy's grinning face, and with her lunatic hair flattened and tamed, it was possible to see the beauty she had once possessed. Might still, if she cared to. The two women called to each other as they floated and dipped beneath the slow, gentle waves, the blissful cold of it.

They lay resting in the great strong arms of the sea.

Jude, too, felt the pull of the ocean, its great rejoicing, dismissing force, but she had not worn her swimsuit. And that was good, for something stronger in her still resisted. Even more, since Sylvie had died, she knew she was not like them; she had not their capacity for abandon, for sharing. Even in that magical tide, this golden light. From the shore she watched.

CHAPTER SEVEN

Drying her hair after her shower, Adele made a leisurely inspection of the other women's toiletry bags. A shared bathroom was where private vulnerabilities were revealed. There were no secrets about the body at this age, but still you sometimes learned things, opening a drawer or a medicine cabinet. Or taking a tiny peek into a toiletry bag. You learned things, like who took Valium, who had constipation . . . small, human things. It made it easier to be kind when you knew things like this.

Jude's voice came from down the hall, calling for Adele to hurry up.

"One minute," she sang back, parting the mouth of Jude's quilted black cosmetics bag to see an array of expensive-looking tubes and squat glass jars. She took a dark blue bottle and squirted a bit of its contents ("skin caviar," she thought it said; that couldn't possibly be right, but she didn't have her glasses) into her palm and then smoothed it over her face with gentle fingers. It smelled delicious. Hopefully Jude wouldn't notice. She took one more little blob and then tossed it back into the bag. There were other, medical-looking white plastic bottles, but the print on the labels was too small to read.

Wendy's toiletry bag was purple and enormous, splotched with smudges of toothpaste. It revealed blister-packed sheets of Phenergan and Claratyne without their boxes, a few decayed foil nubs of aspirin, a bottle of cheap shampoo (but no conditioner, which might explain the state of Wendy's hair), a packet of cotton swabs, some eardrops in a dark brown bottle, a tube of Anusol—Adele quickly let that drop—and several large plastic tubs of cut-price bulk painkillers—Panadol Osteo, ibuprofen, Mersyndol, Imigran—plus squashed-up tubes of toothpaste and more than one toothbrush with their bristles flattened and splayed. There was nothing for Adele in here; she pushed the bag closed.

Jude waited on the sofa. At last Adele appeared in the living room, dewy and pink faced, her abundant blond hair in a messy bun. Wendy was still clumping about in her room, making fossicking sounds with plastic bags.

Jude felt it was rather boastful of Adele to have quite so much hair. It was the kind seen in promotions for retirement living, the ads pretending that growing old could be anything but contemptible. Older women were allowed in advertising now, but only if they were forty-year-olds with silver hair and only if the hair was like Adele's: thick, extravagantly long, and loosely gathered, as if the woman had just emerged from an afternoon of lovemaking with a tanned, muscular man whose own silver hair was as short as hers was long. Jude had even seen a T-shirt worn by a slender young thing—she might have been fifty—at the art gallery. It said OLD IS THE NEW BLACK. But old wasn't the new black if your fluffy thin hair let your scalp show through. It seemed to Jude that it was the dyeing of the skin on her scalp that mattered as much now as the coloring of the hair itself.

Wendy finally appeared in the doorway, holding the big brown leather sack that was her handbag. The three women assessed one another approvingly. Adele wore one of her pretty Indian smocks, printed in a vaguely Islamic design, in bright turquoise and white. They wore jewelry, soft lipstick. They were glad to be leaving the house, entering the world. The sea had rinsed away the afternoon's tensions, even for Jude, who had not swum. Now that it was cooler, it had been agreed they would walk to dinner.

Wendy straightened her back then and, readying for an argument, took a breath to speak. Adele cut in, "It's all right, Wend, we can tie him up somewhere outside the restaurant," at the same time giving Jude a sharp look.

There was no point in arguing. The dog was waiting, staring in at them from the veranda. Jude was careful not to look at his face. She said simply that they had better get going then, because the walk would now take three times as long.

It was still warm, but the lowering sun's heat was diffused by the crests of moving clouds. They took the inclinator—first Jude on her own, holding her breath and gripping the rail while Adele scampered down the stairs, then Wendy and Finn, who shivered and moaned until the motor stopped.

At the bottom the wall on the verge was lined with a row of shiny black bags stuffed with Sylvie's rubbish, their bright yellow handles tied like presents. There was a broken wooden chair and a cracked plastic tub full of things. Jude had written PLEASE TAKE on a piece of cardboard and propped it in the tub, but nobody had taken the decaying hot-water bottle, the pink plastic tray for heart-shaped ice cubes, the rusted barbecue tongs with the ugly wooden handles, the splintery straw bread basket. Of course nobody wanted these depressing old things. Who would?

They stepped out into the street, and Wendy remembered it was Christmastime. She had just about forgotten. School had finished; kids traipsed the streets in groups of three and four, boys shouting swear words and running at one another, girls shrieking.

Finn limped along beside Wendy, agonizingly slowly. She made sure he could walk on the grassy edge of the road. The women dawdled, three abreast on the wide, flat street, the black asphalt emanating warmth beneath their feet. They passed houses with red baubles strung along fences, potted firs ringed with tinsel leaning in the middle of front lawns. In the windows of some houses there were cheap plastic blow-up Santas and reindeer. The grander, more fashionable houses resisted decoration, except that here and there a string of starred white lights was strung taut with joyless elegance across a window.

They reached the strip of shops, where the windows had fat loops of tinsel and glittery Christmas greetings (Wendy snorted: **Happy Holidays.** Americans!), and at the restaurant up ahead the outdoor tables were already dotted with the rosy glow of small red tea candles. The bay shone bright silver. “Oh, wait!” called Adele. “I want to take a photo.”

They stopped while Adele extracted her phone, then turned toward the bay, holding the phone out, shifting for the view, smiling for her own camera.

“Oh, God,” Jude said quietly.

Wendy looked and saw. “Oh, shit,” she said.

You could tell it was her from the carriage of her body, the turban of bright white hair. Ahead on the path, coming toward them, was Sonia Dreyfus.

“Lord,” breathed Wendy. They both turned to see what Adele would do, but she was still behind them, mercifully fiddling with her phone. She had not seen the promenade in progress on the boardwalk: Sonia gliding, regal, with a tall young man, a stooping attendant, by her side.

“Oh, bloody **hell,**” murmured Jude in added horror, “and she’s got her pet boy with her.”

The restaurant door was a few feet away. Jude and Wendy agreed with a glance:

if they could keep Adele looking at her phone, it might be possible to steer her swiftly past the couple and into the restaurant before she noticed them. They slowed a little for Adele to catch up, for them each to take an elbow, but at that exact moment Adele dropped her phone into her handbag and looked up, directly into the faces of Sonia Dreyfus and Joe Gillespie. It was too late.

She made a surprised squawk as Sonia cried out in her deep theatrical voice, “Adele!”

A sort of flapping took place—Wendy thought of geese landing in water—as the two parties met. Wendy’s and Jude’s bodies kept traveling, hoping to carry Adele along in their current, let her call good-bye over her shoulder, retain her dignity.

But no. Adele had stopped and taken a sharp breath, was drawing herself up to face Sonia. Wendy imagined she could see Adele’s heart pulsing beneath her breastbone.

Only yesterday, on the way out of the

city, Wendy had seen this face staring majestically down at her from the back of a bus. DREYFUS. in red capitals, IS. in smaller, slanted gray capitals, then, in stark white, ARKADINA. **Joe Gillespie, Director** was in slightly smaller lettering, and then, beneath that, the play's title, as if an afterthought, **The Seagull.** A few weeks ago, the women had cheerfully derided the production together—a modern adaptation, one of Gillespie's appalling rewrites. They'd heard it was set in contemporary Sydney. Seagull was the name of a media company. There was apparently a lot of cocaine, and Arkadina was sexually involved with her son. Cunnilingus was said to be graphically mimed, and one of the (two) Ninas was played by a man. Six people had walked out of the first performance.

Wendy thought that on the poster Sonia Dreyfus did not look seventy-one; she looked magnificent. But Adele hated Sonia Dreyfus, so Wendy and Jude loyally did, too. This had gone on for thirty-seven years.

Once, a long time ago, Wendy confessed to Jude that she'd seen Dreyfus as Cleopatra. "She is good, don't you think?" she'd asked Jude. She didn't say Sonia's performance had been transporting, miraculous. Even so, Jude had given her a sideways look that meant yes, but to say so was traitorous. "Adele is better" was all she said, and Wendy quickly agreed.

And now here was poor Adele smiling, here was Sonia's solicitous hand on her arm.

It was surprising to Wendy how tiny Sonia was. She was a hairless little monkey: her mouth a thin line, drawn-on eyebrows high and fine, and her pale skin stretched tight over her brow and cheekbones. Her skin was as mottled as ancient parchment. You could push a hole in it with the touch of a finger.

Beside her hung skeletal Joe Gillespie, like a junkie son she'd just collected from the methadone clinic. He wore black rubber thongs on his feet, dirty charcoal jeans, and what looked like a woman's purple silk blouse stretched tight across his bony, sparsely haired chest. He let a weak, uninterested smile float down over the space occupied by Adele and her friends and pulled his limp black hair from one side of his neck to the other.

Was it true that Sonia Dreyfus and **enfant** Gillespie had long had a thing? Was that conceivable? It was repellently intriguing. Wendy imagined him and Sonia wrestling slowly on a bed, one insect carefully devouring another.

Sonia now put her hand to the young man's chest. "Joseph, you know Adele Antoniades, of course," she said.

Gillespie made a movement of his head, indicating thoughtful consideration, and then his smile fixed itself. "Of course I do—**huge** fan." He looked into Adele's eyes, shaking his head reverentially. "Your Martha . . . unforgettable."

Adele beamed and began unfurling into the praise, but Wendy and Jude stared.

Adele had played Martha thirty years ago; Gillespie could have been only ten at the time, if that.

Jude stepped coolly into the conversation, introducing herself and Wendy, seizing power. Jude did look tall sometimes, Wendy thought.

Sonia ignored them, still beaming at Adele, and drove in the knife. "What are you up to now, darling? Teaching? They're lucky to have you."

Wendy was mesmerized. She had suggested teaching to Adele years ago herself, but Adele's scorn had been withering. Teaching meant you were finished and you knew it, she'd sneered. Only failures **taught.** Then she'd seen Wendy's face and added hastily that she meant only in acting.

Sonia clearly held the same view. But it was a mystery to Wendy, standing here, why this woman would want to insult Adele. Sonia had already won: for decades now she'd gotten every part going for a woman over forty. Gillespie cast her in just about everything he did, commissioned works specially for her. What had Adele ever done to Sonia? Wendy felt a loyal fury rising. And as for Joseph and his amazing Technicolor Oedipus complex—but Wendy felt a nudge from Jude, which made her realize her anger must be audible in her breathing. All she could think now was how quickly they could get a drink into Adele once they had her in the restaurant.

Adele had looked away, but now she met Sonia's gaze and laughed lightly in a way that returned Sonia's insult. "Oh, good God, no, I have absolutely no interest in teaching," she said. She let a silence follow, offering them nothing. She knew the power of the pause. Wendy could see that it was unnerving them.

An unpleasant little smile began at Gillespie's lips. "So," he said, challenging her. "What are you working on?"

Adele was watching Finn, who stood on the footpath, waiting. Wendy saw his sad, dignified body, his long, grubby face. He stared blankly out at the street, unmoved by all the human need and strain above him. Adele turned back to Gillespie. "Nothing," she said.

The shock, the wound of it. Adele never admitted a lack of work to anyone, ever, always choosing from her collection of stock lines about projects in development, irons in fires. She had told a humiliating truth. Wendy resisted reaching out to take her arm.

But Adele was not finished. She squinted at the bay and said simply, "To be honest, I really can't think of anyone I want to work with just now."

Wendy and Jude caught each other's glance. "Anyone" meant directors. Artistic directors, of major theater companies, like Joe Gillespie. Which meant that this Adele, uninterested in work, was acting right now, superbly. It was kind of thrilling.

"I mean," she went on regretfully—as though all this were obvious, between friends—"have you seen anything decent lately? Anything with something real, something fresh, to say?"

Sonia kept her cool, but Gillespie was no actor. He shriveled in affront.

Adele's breasts stood their ground. Sonia tried to keep smiling, but even she couldn't keep it up; she stared at Adele now with open contempt. But this new, liberated Adele did not receive Sonia's hostile glare. She was digging in her handbag to extract her sunglasses; she drew them out and put them on. "That sun is still really very hot," she said.

Jude took charge then, ignoring Gillespie completely and luring Sonia in with her old maître d's disdain, an expert combination of superiority and boredom, that forced Sonia to try to impress her. They always came to Bittoes for Xander's orphan's Christmas, said Sonia, gesturing toward Louisa Crescent, where all the houses were enormous, with fancy views. Jude made no response, expressionless. Though of course Xander wasn't here this year, Sonia tried; he was in Idaho filming with Woody Harrelson. Jude still showed no interest, but Sonia persisted, laughing lightly about "the kids" in their group, the famed young starlets from theater and film. She began reeling off their celebrity My Little Pony names—Abby, Toby, Sophy—but Jude cut her off with a wide, brutal smile and a wave of her hand.

"Actors' names are lost on me, I'm afraid," she said. Then she was sorry, they were late for their dinner booking, Wendy you must tie that dog up, Merry Christmas.

Jude and Adele stepped through the restaurant doors, and Wendy turned away to a streetlight pole. It was smooth as a ballet, and Sonia and Gillespie were left standing alone on the footpath.

Wendy looped Finn's leash around the pole, marveling at Jude and at Adele's transformation. She saw Dreyfus and Gillespie marooned in the street. They were not accustomed to being the ones left, did not know how to do it. Wendy was proud of her rude, clever, undaunted friends.

Then a threesome of people at an outdoor table called out to Sonia, and Wendy saw her expand, grow queenly once more at the sound of her name. One of the men passed his phone to Gillespie, who stepped back to take the picture while the fan club posed, laughing excitably, gathering Sonia between them. She dropped a coquettish shoulder to pose with her admirers, and once the photograph was taken, she stood with them a moment, soaking up the avid attention of the sort of people to whom the name Adele Antoniades would mean nothing.

Wendy looked into the restaurant, where Adele, shaking her hair and laughing with Jude in the halogen light, had no idea she'd already been vanquished.

Wendy patted Finn. In the softening light, he seemed to her somehow valiant and enduring, despite his frailty. There was something noble in his bearing just now, and she thumped his skinny flank rhythmically, lovingly, as she watched Queen Sonia proceeding down the boardwalk. And then she saw something else. Gillespie, unsmiling, moved off to inspect something in the lit window of the gift shop. As he turned his back on Sonia, Wendy saw the vigor drain from her body. Her face, as she stood waiting for him, was no longer proud. She looked exhausted, and lost. Then Gillespie issued a curt word without looking at her and strode on, moving fast on his long legs. Sonia trotted alongside him, trying to keep up.

Jude scanned the room to find someone who would bring them a drink, but the restaurant was in chaos. There was no glassware or cutlery on the table, and both the young waitresses had vanished as soon as she and Adele reached their table. What she craved now was a good martini, but that would not be possible here. Locals' Night: the words made her shudder. The menu promised the blend of pretentiousness and incompetence shared by too many regional restaurants. **Fresh bread will be served complimentary after ordering.**

She would rather an honest pub meal than this truffled wagyu rubbish.

She sounded like Catherine and Michael. A bit of plain food, was that too much to ask? They spoke fondly of Meals on Wheels, though you couldn't call that food. Criminal, Jude thought. You got malnourished, exhausted, vulnerable elderly people and told them they should be grateful for a tray of hot slop left on the doorstep, and then you wondered why they went mad or brain dead.

It was **not** hot slop, Michael had barked once, one of the very few times since childhood she'd seen him angry. It was perfectly good roasted meat and vegetables. **What a snob you are,** he'd said bitterly. **You're no more special than anyone else.** She'd said nothing, only raised her eyebrows and apologized coolly for offending him. But inside, shameful, fierce, Jude thought, **Oh, yes I am.**

She always thought of Michael and Catherine as belonging to a previous generation, though her brother was only five years older and Catherine was the same age as Jude herself. What was it? The friends had discussed this, when Sylvie was alive, how oddly some people seemed more part of your parents' generation than your own. Sylvie said it was the obsession with doctors. For a while they agreed: all four women despised doctors and went only when absolutely necessary. They refused prescribed pharmaceuticals—at least they told one another they did—and scorned people they knew who'd turned their ailments into a hobby, who lived their lives in waiting rooms, were competitive about their specialists, having test after test after test. Adele and Jude and Wendy and Sylvie despised those women, whose idea of conversation had shrunk to recitations of their blood-lipid levels or bone-density counts.

But Michael and Catherine were not so much like this; it wasn't to do with the body. It wasn't even the conservatism, though that was part of it.

It was Wendy who diagnosed the difference: "The problem is the inner life," she declared. "Your brother has none. Nor does his wife."

Jude pointed out that Michael subscribed to the symphony and had season tickets to the theater, that they hobbled along (that was cruel, but Catherine's back was beginning to curve with compression fractures and osteoporosis; Jude had no sympathy) to openings at the art gallery and bookish events. They were patrons of this and that charity and research facility and festival.

"Doesn't matter if you still don't know how to think," Wendy had said.

After that, Jude listened more carefully to Catherine's and Michael's descriptions of what they heard and saw. They listed events and venues and who was playing the lead, directing, conducting, speaking. If you asked them what they thought of it, they couldn't say, beyond "Oh, **marvelous**" if Sonia Dreyfus or Elsa Blake was in it or "**Very** impressive" if the actor was a man they knew from television. Catherine's book club worked doggedly through the Booker short list, coming down on the side of the winner if they knew the author already, against if they didn't.

Occasionally Jude prodded Catherine or Michael on something specific, some detail about the production or the novel—she'd heard the lighting was distracting, or the script fell away in the middle, or the prose was overblown. They answered in vague, uncomfortable terms and then looked at her suspiciously, as if she were trying to catch them out. Which she was.

This was the sort of moment when Catherine would begin to talk about something practical, something that provoked no dangerous opinions. Holidays, perhaps, or gardening. She might ask, with a little acid in her voice, "Back at the what's-it-called—**ashram**—for Christmas again this year, Jude?" and they would go through the usual charade. Catherine wasn't stupid, inner life or no inner life.

When Michael sensed this bristle of friction between the two women, he retreated into a distracted silence with a strange half smile stuck on his face.

Was this what getting old was made of? Routines and evasions, boring yourself to death with your own rigid judgments? Visiting her brother and his wife in their cavernous house in the leafy suburb pulled Jude a little closer, each time, to death. She could feel it.

On evenings like these, with the stifling air of their lush green garden pressing into her lungs, she would kiss them good bye a little earlier than usual—she felt her brother's dry, pecking dart at her face, the relief visible in his shoulders as he waved from the step—and she would be sure to walk with a straight back to her car, pretending her body moved as fluidly as it had done in her youth, without the stiffness, without the familiar licks of pain flickering along her spine. She wanted them to see how very unlike them she was, to feel the contrast of her French linen pants and fine silk cardigan against Catherine's ironed pink T-shirts and navy skirts.

Jude knew she had cruelty in her, but she didn't care. She would reverse swiftly, a little recklessly, down their long driveway, swivel out onto the wide silent street, and turn her sleek black Audi for the bridge, the city, home.

Now she looked up from the menu and found that wineglasses and a bottle of adequate Riesling had appeared, and so had Wendy, and Adele was settling back into her seat.

"I charmed them." Adele winked.

How had Jude missed this? Sometimes it shocked her a little, that things could go by, could happen on the physical plane in which her body sat, but she did not perceive them taking place.

Once Wendy had said, carefully not looking in her direction, "Of course, some people have too much inner life. You still have to live in the world, in your body. . . ." Their eyes had met, and then

Wendy looked away, noncommittally. "That's what I think anyway."

That's what Sylvie thought, too. It was why she arrived at Wendy's with the puppy, to force her outside, into the world. There were other reasons as well, but Sylvie had been right about Finn. He did force Wendy to wake, eat, move. It might have saved her life.

Wendy had the dog, but Jude had nothing. Except she had the thing nobody else would ever understand. It had come to Jude long ago that the only time she felt fully present in the world—when the membrane between her and living was actually permeable and that nourishment of every kind could pass through, that she could be contributing worth to the world as well as drawing from it—was when she was with Daniel.

At first it was a shock to understand this. But soon it made sense of everything, of the way she lived her life. She went about the world, in the times Daniel was not with her, in what she thought of now as the pre-expressive or aggregation phase. Gathering experience, formulating opinions, developing ideas, trying out recipes and restaurants. Getting things out of the way: shopping, household chores. Absorbing things—events and politics and aesthetics, reading and observing and analyzing and then folding into herself these things she had read and seen and thought. And then, when Daniel presented himself at her door—once a week, or once a month—she would feel both a bodily and an intellectual relaxation, when all the complexity of what she had seen and done and thought about in the preceding weeks would move through her, and she was ready to integrate these things into her character, rejecting this, selecting that. It was as though Daniel were a kind of trigger mineral, his presence essential for the absorption of all the other spiritual and intellectual and physical nutrients gathered, but unintegrated, inside her.

Of course they had broken up. Of course she had tried with other men, would have at times accepted a lesser person. But after several listless attempts—it never worked—she gave in. She would rather be alone with the gathering force of all this inside her, never to be released, than be forced up against the sheer, dull block of not-Daniel.

Now she looked at her friends and saw that in the dusky light coming through the window and the glimmering candle on the table between them that they were beautiful. This surprise, too, she would fold away and save for Daniel. Two more days.

Was that true, Adele? What you said to Gillespie?" asked Wendy, once the bread basket arrived and they'd begun a second glass of wine.

Adele smiled, tipping back her wine.

Jude snorted on her behalf. "Of course not! But he's never going to cast her. Why give them the satisfaction of thinking she wants it?"

They looked to Adele for confirmation. She held the wine in her mouth a moment, nodded, swallowed. She supposed this was right; Jude usually was. But also, something had happened on the footpath there with Finn staring so plainly at the street and the bay. She looked past the women now through the window, and they leaned as well, to see Finn sitting by the pole on the path, front paws neatly together. He did not look around for Wendy but gazed quietly into the air before him. It was this Adele had seen. His simple creatureliness.

She didn't understand it herself.

She waved the subject away and said, "Do you ever hear from Sylvie?"

Their skeptical gazes—first Jude's, then Wendy's—settled upon her.

"I do," she said happily. This would annoy them, but it was true, like on the train today when Sylvie had spoken firmly to her. Jude would call this frontal-lobe damage. She called all mysterious things frontal-lobe damage.

Surprisingly, Jude did not roll her eyes.

She looked hesitant, as if she might say something, but changed her mind. "Frontal-lobe damage," she said, and glanced down at the menu.

"You order," said Adele placidly. She actually fancied the fish and chips, but this would displease Jude, who would order them something restrained and healthy—like ceviche of kingfish or a green papaya salad, and Adele would be hungry later, and it would still be more expensive than the fish and chips. But this was how it was. Restaurants were Jude's world, and you did not argue.

Adele looked at her across the table now in her fine black linen, sitting straight in her seat, alert and handsome. Now and then she leaned forward ever so slightly, watching you as you spoke. It had only dawned on Adele recently that Jude's hearing was going, but she would never lower herself to ask you to repeat something. Adele thought that these days Jude was lip-reading as much as hearing. She could not imagine her deigning to get a hearing aid. She realized, with surprise, that she felt sorry for Jude. Jude! Who had always been strongest, who could hurt you the most.

She could have been an actor, Adele knew. A fine one. A great one, perhaps, certainly better than Adele. Jude knew it, too, though it had never been spoken. The knowledge lay between them, always had, from the first time Jude went to a performance by Adele. Early on she would give Adele tight little compliments, praising some small, highly specific detail of her performance but never the whole. As time went on, they would meet in the foyer afterward for a drink, and Jude felt entitled to dissect the production, smiling as she demolished the various elements—lighting, stagecraft, score, Adele's fellow actors—as if these had nothing to do with Adele, as if the two women were in obvious agreement. And never flattering Adele herself, who mostly left those evenings swallowing down tears, because Jude was like a reverse Midas, walking through your life pointing at the things you cherished, one, two, three, and at her touch each one turned to shit.

But when she praised you . . . well, it meant something, to have Jude's good opinion.

Ray used to say Jude didn't have friends, she had subordinates. Which was true, perhaps, when they were young. But all that had broken away at some point. When? It was hard to remember.

People thought Adele was indestructible, superficial. But sometimes, when she looked back, her entire life appeared to her as a river of hurt, rushing and rushing. Torrents of painful things: slights, rejections, curt words, reviews, smiling insults, failed auditions, glances across tables.

The professional hurts slowly faded, but the intimate ones, inflicted by her friends, lingered. All the times Wendy and Jude and Sylvie had dinners together without her and phoned each other for the long and intimate chats she knew they had, or the times they met in New York or Nice or Rome for their holidays while Adele was too broke to go anywhere, miserably waiting for the next gig.

But then somehow the part of you that was the sandbank, your edges eroding from resisting all this hurt, that part just broke away and was swept down, and all of life was the river. And you went with it.

That's what Adele thought now, looking at Jude with her little skullcap of fine dark hair and her crooked crimson mouth, her long nose with its delicate carved nostrils flaring when she was displeased, like at this moment, about the bread. Soon she would call the waitress over in her deep, throaty voice. Jude had **presence,** which was the thing everyone had said about her back in her restaurant days, when she was the power people's darling, when getting a table at Pellini's or the Boardroom or the Waterside while Jude was in control became a personal achievement. When she took command of a room with a slow turn of her head, the charge of that gaze.

The bread seemed perfectly fine to Adele and Wendy, who chewed stolidly, but not to Jude. "It's **stale,**" she said to them, as if they were both fools. She turned in her seat to beckon the waitress.

What **were** all those hurts, back then? Adele couldn't remember, though there was a time when she would keep track of every one. She would store them up and **ponder them in her heart.** Was that the expression? Something biblical. Whenever she was lonely or miserable, back then, she would take them out and count them: all the times she'd been slighted or patronized, the times she sat in the toilet crying while her dearest friends laughed together and talked, so avid, so brave, and Adele was an ugly little mouse hiding in the toilet weeping. It gave her a sort of comfort, back then, to feel she'd been wronged. There was something exhilarating, life-giving almost, in the depth of that feeling. There were fights and phone calls, vengeful letters, condemnations and accusations. It was all so exhausting when you looked back. However did they have the energy? They were all mad!

It was the drinking, the children, the drugs, the affairs, she supposed. It was the ambition and the failure. The teetering marriages, the envy, the cycles of paucity and wealth. It was the times. Then the departures and returns, the cautious reunions, the never-quite-complete forgiveness. And now it was all so long in the past that Adele could never remember what any of it had ever been **about,** except that they were simply too young, even when middle-aged, and much too full of feeling.

She took up her glass, swigged a gulp of wine, and watched Jude, who had stuck up for her against Sonia and Gillespie. **Jude wouldn't piss on you if you were on fire** was another thing Ray used to say, but that wasn't true. And look how he turned out; Jude had had his number from the start.

"Did you see that a doctor was charged with murdering his mother this morning?"

Jude said then. "She was eighty-eight. He's sixty-one."

They looked at Wendy, and Adele joked that she'd better watch out.

"Nobody cares enough to want to murder **us,**" Adele said to Jude. They clinked their wineglasses in childless solidarity. In fact, for a time in her thirties, Adele had wanted a baby very badly. Her friends had been through the miscarriages with her, again and again. Wendy was by far the kindest.

The waitress appeared, a little breathless, a flopping Santa hat pinned to her hair. She wore tiny white shorts, and her legs were long, golden, glorious. Adele wanted to reach out and run a hand up that luscious thigh. The girl smiled down at them, the sequins of her red tank top glinting. "What can I do for you ladies?" She laid a hand lightly on Jude's upper arm as she spoke, which was a mistake.

Jude pointed at the bread. "This is stale. Can you bring us some fresh bread, please?"

The girl cocked her head, and her smile

grew kinder. **Oh, no,** Adele wanted to tell her. **Don't do what you are going to do.** There was a subtle, dangerous shift in Jude's posture as the young woman poked a strand of long golden hair behind her ear and bent down, resting her hands on her knees as you might do when speaking to a preschooler. She beamed and said sweetly to Jude, just a little too loudly, "Oh, I know what you mean, but this is **sour**-dough bread? It's just a kind of a different texture to what you might be used to?"

Jude reclined, ever so slightly, and met the girl's eyes with her cold, neutral gaze. Wendy and Adele looked at each other, then at the table, and Wendy swallowed down a big lump of bread as Jude said in a low voice, "I know what sourdough bread is." She held the basket out to the girl, then said slowly, again—this time subtly parodying the girl's patronizing tone, "But **this** bread is stale."

The restaurant noise swelled around them, and the waitress's smile turned to bewilderment. She caught Adele's and

Wendy's expressions then, and under Jude's stare she blushed, looked suddenly as if she might cry. She snatched up the basket and whirled away into the clatter of cutlery and the peals of other people's laughter.

Wendy watched the girl twisting and pushing her way through the tables, bread basket held high, and thought about what could have happened to provoke a sixty-one-year-old son into murdering his mother. She thought about all that suffering, thought about what she had not thought about in years.

It was all right to take part in the delusions of children but not adults, and you were not supposed to tell a person he was crazy. So when Jamie was five and said he was a train driver, that was good, but when he was nineteen and said he was the prime minister, locked in his car, locked in the psych ward, you couldn't say, **That's ridiculous,** you had to say, **Your thoughts**

seem a little disordered. You had to ask gentle, probing questions, like **Where is your office, who are your staff, how did you become the prime minister since last week when you were a student driving a delivery van,** and you were supposed to be glad to see the confusion, to see every speck of confidence draining out of his beautiful young face. And then he wrote down some song lyrics on a piece of paper torn from Wendy's notebook, and he cried softly while he was doing it, and then he stopped crying and said he was the prime minister again.

He'd looked at Wendy in the hospital garden—they called it a garden—sucking and sucking on cigarettes, and he said, "You've tried, but you've made a lot of mistakes." He shook his head in resignation, an old-timer lamenting a newcomer's lack of basic skills, but he was talking about Wendy being a mother. He exhaled her failure in one long plume of smoke. "A **lotta** mistakes." A pale young man had drifted peacefully past them in the garden and Jamie said, "Don't look at him he's a fucking psycho, did you bring me more cigarettes?"

Jamie was fine now; that was only a brief and horrifying period in his twenties, and then he finished university and moved to London and got a boyfriend and then moved to Stuttgart and became a technician in a laser eye clinic, and two years ago he married his boyfriend (there was no wedding, he told Wendy, there was nothing to be invited **to**), and then they moved to Prague. And they were happy and Jamie never went mad again. How did that happen? Jamie would be fifty next year. How did that happen?

He never went mad again, but about two years before Lance died, Claire had suddenly gone to see Jamie in Stuttgart, just for a week, leaving Philip and baby Max at home. It was just a holiday! She'd repeated this so emphatically that Wendy knew it wasn't true. And when, in a vulnerable moment, Wendy had idiotically revealed to Claire what Jamie had said all those years ago, she looked uncomfortable, and there was a silence, and then she said woodenly, "I'm sure you were doing your best with what you had at the time, Mum," and changed the subject.

What was that supposed to mean?

Wendy had never confessed these things to her friends. She'd complained gaily about her kids many times, of course, but never admitted these deepest, most incomprehensible injuries. **A** lotta **mistakes. I'm sure you did your best.** "What's done is done," her own mother used to say grimly. But that was something you said after things had gone wrong or someone had made a stupid mistake. And what could Wendy have done wrong?

At the table Jude and Adele were on a cheerful roll now, listing ageist crimes committed against them lately by girls in shops, men on buses.

"And she says to me," said Adele, "'Do

you know someone who could show you how to use a computer? There's a thing called **Google**?'"

They hooted with righteous contempt. Jude produced a fresh instance of her particular favorite, a podiatrist telling her how much she loved old people, because—and Adele joined in, singing it—"you have such wonderful **stories**!"

Normally Wendy would join in, too, for God knew she had a vast collection of her own—that child from the university press emailing last week, so happy to know Wendy was still out and about! Or the moronic pharmacist, calling her "young lady" and **winking**—but tonight she said nothing. She felt sorry for the little waitress, and Jude was a bully, and what did a bit of stale bread matter anyway?

There was a loud chime, and as Adele chattered on, Wendy saw Jude pull out her phone, read a message, and hide a tiny smile, tap a quick reply, and drop it back in her bag.

Outside, Finn sat by his pole. Wendy wanted the comfort of his rough, hairy body against her bare leg. She tried to meet his line of sight through the window, but he could not see her. Tied to a pole, lost in his blind, deaf, animal world.

CHAPTER EIGHT

There was a scuffling outside Wendy's bedroom door in the middle of the night. She was seized with panic but then realized it couldn't be Finn, locked out on the deck where she had heard his clicking paws over the boards for most of the night. But still, she threw off the sheet and went to make sure. Through that glass door, she made out his shaggy form, finally exhausted, asleep at the base of her door in the pale moonlight.

The scuffling continued: it was in the house. A rat?

Opening her bedroom door and peering out, she saw Adele halfway down the dark hall. What was she doing? The bathroom was on the other side of the house.

She saw that Adele was at the linen closet in the corridor, stooping and clawing, trying to find a handle. Did she think the closet was a toilet?

Wendy whispered loudly, but not enough to wake Jude, "Adele. You all right?"

Adele fell still, openmouthed, frowning into the darkness between them. Wendy was sorry to have startled her. She looked frail, the sagging T-shirt of her nightdress glowing white in the darkness. It was not clear that she could see Wendy, or had even heard her. Wendy had moved to go to her when abruptly she grunted something, a sound or a word Wendy could not make out, and turned away, shuffling back down the hall.

Wendy watched her slow retreat and waited until she heard her ascend the stairs to her own room. Then she returned to her bed and lay there, staring out through the window at the dark, starry sky.

She woke again, much later, to Finn's high whine coming in through the doorframe. She was grateful for Jude's growing deafness, prayed she had not heard it. He was whimpering at the veranda post. She slipped outside, got herself down to sit on the boards, and called him to her. He turned, staring at her in the same way he peered at the post. But then he recognized her and fell on her, pawing and whining. As she patted him, he lifted his face—baffled, betrayed—to stare into her eyes. "It's okay, Finny Fin," she whispered, rubbing and thumping his long, skinny back.

There was a noise from around the corner, and then she saw Adele letting herself out of the house, pattering down the wooden steps in her exercise clothes. She was no longer the stooped, lost ghost Wendy had seen in the dark hallway but transformed back into herself. Wendy would not embarrass her by asking about her movements in the night. She watched how she moved now, her quick stride out into the street, the motion of her muscled little body, bustling with purpose and direction.

Finn began licking the back of her hand, obsessively, and she let him, watching the skin of her own wrist sliding and releasing with the motion of his tongue. Eventually it became uncomfortable, rasping, and she pulled her hand away. Again the mystified, betrayed tilt of his head.

She needed to pee but did not want him to begin his whining again. If she could only bring him inside with her. But Jude would be out of bed soon, and already there was a puddle on the veranda boards. Finn quite often pissed himself now, when he slept. Or worse. Usually Wendy found it quickly and dispatched the little lumps, or the hospital pads took care of it, but Claire had found that little patch of yellowing dried shit under her desk. Cruel, she'd said. But what was cruel about letting the natural body do what it must? Cruelty would be punishing him for these small accidents.

That nurse who had been filmed laying into the old man in the nursing home, lunging at him with a shoe, got six months' home detention. It was awful, the grainy footage from the camera hidden by the family. The hopeless wavering of the elderly man, the flailing savagery of the young one, tearing at his clothes. The newspapers showed the nurse in beautiful Indian ceremonial dress at a wedding with his wife and baby, their faces blurred. What had happened to fill him with such rage?

Wendy was already sweaty. She wanted a shower, needed the hot water on her stiff shoulder. She made her way onto her hands and knees and then, with the aid of the post, got up from the boards, whispering to Finn, "Don't worry, I'll be back." But he had already begun again, up and down the boards, **tick-tick-tick.**

As the light in the bedroom turned gauzy in the hour before dawn and the first bird gave out its lonely cry, Adele dressed, pulling on a pair of Liz's cool, shiny leggings and letting the elastic snap at her waist. She sat on the closed toilet seat and pushed her feet into her walking shoes, and then she took her phone and fingered a five-dollar note from Wendy's wallet on the countertop before slipping out, down the sets of stairs, into the street.

In the darkness of the early morning, walking the streets on Christmas Eve, she felt especially alive to the world. Her skin was soft in the humidity and her footfall confident, moving without hesitation along the quiet road. The little town opened itself to Adele in this secret hour, the scent of frangipani drawing forth a vivid sense of possibility from her dreaming hours into the day.

There was nobody on the streets. Far off she heard a truck grinding along the highway, but no cars passed as she walked, and there were only a few soft lights in windows here and there. It was the holidays, and too early for almost everyone.

She would take the shortcut, making her way along the streets past the tall quiet houses, along the footpath to the steep carved stairway down to the small park on the bay, where she would rest for a time on the low wall, listening to the slock of the water against the stone.

At this time of the day, Adele was free from the past, free of the future. Her body grew more sinuous as she walked, the morning stiffness in her limbs dissolving. She considered her body; she thought of it as her oldest friend. She thought about her fascia, the miraculous satiny sheath covering all her muscles, a single coating of astonishing stretchy plastic encasing her entire body's musculature beneath the skin, and it slid and glided as she moved. Adele's imagined fascia was colored a beautiful gunmetal gray. It gleamed with movement. On these silent morning walks, her body was ageless, it had seen no degradation. Her skin was taut and smooth over her limbs, she felt it shining under the fading moon and the pale orange streetlights, her fluid satin fascia slithering all over with each movement of her forearms, her hips, her calves. Perspiration came, yes, on her lip and between her breasts, but it was the heady hour of the frangipani and the indigo sky and her own sleepy body, and her deep and opened mind was free to roam without guilt, without strain or regret. Into her mind came her Martha self, her Hedda self, her Desdemona. She was all of these women: Masha, Ophelia, Saint Joan and Linda Loman, Elizabeth Proctor and Blanche DuBois, and as she padded softly along the footpaths of Bittoes, her breath entering and leaving her body with ease, these women surged through Adele, inhabiting her, and she was lit and carried by them. By their joys, their rages and yearnings. There were moments, indeed, when she was all energy, all spirit, the way she'd been in her most transcendent moments on the stage, the women's lives coursing through her. She was all body, and at the same time she possessed no body at all.

Except, resting here at last on the low stone wall, her strong heart pulsing, panting here beside the slopping water, she very much needed to wee.

There were no toilets in the park. The water surface where it met the walls was lined with flotsam, garlands of polystyrene burger boxes and plastic bags, undulating prettily, luminous on the dark water. Strands of pearly rubbish fetched up at the water's edge. She could hold on.

The sun was emerging, but from here she could not see the bright ball itself; the sky was overcast, and the sun had not yet risen above the curve of the headland. She was grateful for the cloud. She pulled at the hem of her T-shirt and used it to wipe her lip, her face. She would sit awhile, waiting for the light on the water, because to see this was beautiful.

The need to pee pressed upon her, annoying. The predawn, dreamy feeling inside her was draining away. But she would hold on. It was good to hold on, in fact, good for the body. For the pelvic floor, which was distasteful to consider. Not distasteful but . . . dispiriting. Like something for old people, though of course all sorts of women had pelvic-floor problems. Still, it was drab to think about. She squeezed. It may be good for the body, but it was bad for the spirit. If it were not for this irritation, Adele could sit here for a long time on the wall, her face turned serenely toward the rising sun. She might appear to be meditating, which she was, in a way. She closed her eyes, her back to the water, and laid the backs of her hands on her knees as she had seen people do. Loosely pinched together her thumb and forefinger. Or was it the second finger? She straightened her spine, here in her slender body and her fresh white T-shirt that lay loosely over her skin. A woman alive, richly experiencing a new morning of her life, here by the water's edge.

There was a hollow, irregular flapping sound and Adele opened her eyes. A small sailboat came into view.

The smell of the bay comforted Adele. She closed her eyes again and summoned the slow, loosened feeling of earlier. A woman alive, who had been many women, but now she **really** needed to pee and suddenly could ignore it no more. The urgency lifted her off her seat, sent her scurrying to the edge of the park, out of sight of the boat, which was moving off in any case. The park was shadowy and silent here in the corner where the stone stairs met the wall, and she was desperate. It could not be helped; in haste she dug her thumbs into the waistband of her leggings and she squatted with her back against the wall, which she expected to be cool, but no, it still held the warmth of the day before. She squatted and was careful, and there was such pleasure, suddenly, in letting go.

Pelvic floor or no. Knees apart, the short squirt of urine emptying quietly, intently, into the grass. Her breath escaped, too, in relief.

It was nothing, as she eased herself up the wall, tugging at her stretchy pants, which were only a little sprinkled. It was simply a moment between Adele and herself and the wall and the grass, in the dawn.

But a movement caught her eye across the park. A small silver flag, which was a little white dog, trotting toward her. Adele's breath jerked, her fingers pulled downward at the T-shirt, tugged down over her thighs, and she was stepping quickly away from the wall, from the place, and there was a man, there was Joe Gillespie turning from the water with a leash in his hand. He had turned to find his dog and was startled by the sight of her, Adele, stepping out of the shadows.

He had not seen her squatting.

He looked at her now across the grass, then turned back to the water. But she could tell he was puzzled by the appearance of this woman—he hadn't recognized her—emerging from the corner of the park in the dawn. It was quite certain he did not see her crouching to piss in the grass, she knew that.

"Good morning," she called airily. She stood there, breathing. She stretched her arms over her head. It was normal, to do yoga in a park.

Gillespie called to his dog, but the little creature, its metal tags tinkling, was snuffling at the grass into which Adele's urine had only just been spilled. The dog's small, triangular black nose was right in there, dampening itself among the blades of pissed-upon grass. For a moment Adele was flooded with shame, and she wanted to kick the dog, savagely, in its soft belly. Soon, she supposed, Gillespie would pick it up in his arms and let its piss-covered nose nuzzle his shirt. She planted her feet apart and lowered herself, arms extended, Warrior Two. Ignoring the sniffing dog, the sweet balloon of its belly. She had never wanted to harm an animal in her life.

Gillespie was looking at her, recognition dawning. She would never harm an animal, but there it was, sniffing, exposing her, with its small scuffling grunts. She wished she'd not said what she'd said to Joe Gillespie on the street last night.

"Oh, hello, Adele," he said. There was hostility in his voice.

"Good morning, Joe," she said, closing her eyes, lowering herself farther, pain in her knee. She knew how to convince, though she felt a little unsteady now, and her pulse shivered. It was hard to keep her arms raised, her leg bent. She believed quite suddenly that it was not safe to be here in the empty park with Gillespie staring at her, his dog sniffing. She had a sensation that her heart had slid somehow out of place inside its cavity, creeping too high in her chest. It was interfering with her breath, which was coming too slowly, or too fast.

Gillespie barked out, "Coco! Come here!" And the dog scampered to him. He bent to clip a lead to the dog's yellow collar. Coco. It must be Sonia's dog.

Adele stayed where she was, began to move into Reverse Warrior. But her arms and her legs were beginning to shake now with the effort. She would not slump to the ground in front of Gillespie, though she wanted to. She remembered that in her dream last night she had offered to cook a lavish dinner for many people, but something had gone wrong. There was a crowded room, a sense of unseemly failure.

Gillespie turned away now, and she let her arms drop and straightened, taking care not to stumble. He walked with the dog to the far end of the park, to the jetty that stuck out into the bay. He leaned over the railing halfway along the wharf, staring into the water, the dog nosing about at the end of the leash.

Her heart had slipped back to its right place in her chest, but it still beat too fast. She looked for the sun, but the cloud had thickened and she could not see where it might be in the whitening sky. It was already humid. She sweated heavily now beneath her T-shirt; a mosquito whined at her ear. The artistic director of the Box Factory Theatre, whom she had already insulted, could surely not have seen her pissing in the grass like a tramp, a bag lady. The feeling from last night—tranquil, simple—was gone. For an irrational moment, she wished she had brought Finn on her walk.

And now Gillespie was striding back down the jetty toward her. She could tell by the speed and direction of his walk that he had something to say to her.

There was a secret, watery part of herself in which Wendy could see the future. She sleepily thought this in the hot morning, though she wasn't really sure what it meant, as she sat drinking her coffee on the deck. She peered down into the fishpond. There were fish in there. Supposed to be fish in there anyway, though the water was dark and there was a film of slime over the leaves of the water lily.

The heat was rising off the wooden decking and the walls of the house. The insect screens sagged, and there looked to be rotting timber in the far back corner of the deck. She could not stand the idea of mentioning this to Jude. It was too hot to think about it. They could just push a planter box across that corner.

It was a morning in which her dreams lay close to the surface. She had dreamed the women were staying in an enormous Italian stone villa, with a drawbridge and servants. And just when it was her turn to go into the great hall—the other two had gone ahead of her—she awoke. As she swam up from sleep, watching them step into the cavernous space, she thought, **They don't even know the history.**

The thing that hurt, she realized on waking, was that she'd not yet reached the place she had always felt was there waiting for her, if she could only work hard enough, if her intellect could stretch just that last, tiniest bit further. A red fish materialized in the water, gliding to the surface. She leaned, watching its purposeful, slow waddle through the murky water. People like Wendy had had their turn; that's what she was supposed to accept now. It was time for her to go away, to step back. The fish reached the water surface. She could see no eyes, but its tiny mouth opened and closed into the air, patiently seeking. Yes. Life—ideas, thinking, experience—was still there, to be mastered, expressed, in the way that only she could do it. She had not finished her turn, would not sink down. She wanted more.

From inside the house came the sounds of crockery and running taps, and then she heard Jude shouting. She got up and scurried down the deck toward the kitchen.

Poor Finn cowered in a corner, shaking. Wendy went to him, cupped his dirty face gently in her hand while she threw a tea towel onto the offending pool on the linoleum.

"Really," Jude hissed, and it seemed to Wendy that Jude, too, was shaking like Finn, not with fear but fury. Not physically but in a cold, forbidding part of herself, inside. That part was always there in Jude; you could feel it waiting for you.

"It's all right," Wendy called calmly, making a little wall around the pool of dog piss with the tea towel, pushing at it with her foot while taking hold of Finn's collar. She was talking to Finn, but she meant it for Jude as well. A tiny bit of wee! You'd think a calamity had happened.

Jude marched across the room and stood over Wendy, dramatically unspooling long yards of paper towel from a roll, and then clamped the roll beneath her elbow, ripping off the paper with unnecessary violence. "Here." She brandished the bouquet at Wendy, who was kneeling now to try to pull Finn toward her. His front legs were rigid, he shook.

"He's terrified," Wendy said. "Shouting at him just makes it worse." He was getting deafer, but he was very sensitive. He could feel aggression in the air, and it frightened him terribly. And Jude's anger was worse than most. Wendy ignored Jude's outstretched hand, let the paper float to the ground.

Jude marched back and forth between fridge and sink and began one of her bouts of relentless counter wiping, leaning with her whole body, muttering martyrishly about how Gail was possibly supposed to sell a house that stank of dog shit and piss. Then she turned and held up a finger. "We agreed he would stay **outside.**"

Wendy got stiffly to her feet. **You agreed,** she thought. But she would not argue with Jude while she was in this mood.

"Come on, Finny," she whispered. She hoped Jude noticed Finn anxiously licking his lips—his stretched black lips, so tender, so loose—and the fact that under the kindness of her own voice his shaking was subsiding. He got to his feet and lumbered across the room, **click-click-click,** to follow her outside.

"I'll clean it away in a minute," she called

back over her shoulder as she and the dog made their way onto the deck and across to the corner where the shade of the pepper tree still fell.

The cicadas slowed and then began again, offering their ceaseless wild shriek to the hot sky. She clipped the lead to Finn's collar and patted him. She went back inside, cleaned up the piss, came out again with her hat and car keys, and said, "Come on, darling, let's go for a walk."

At Adele's gym the young women smiled in a politely bored way when the middle-aged ones marveled at her fitness. She was flexible, could touch her toes, Adele looked great. Adele's little bottom neat in Liz's Lululemon tights, her famous breasts still famous. She was their pet. They gushed, the older ones, about how dazzling Adele had once been (**once**—she ignored that, smiled, she was an actress). They remembered how she'd set the city on fire one summer, she and Jack, **Who's Afraid of Virginia Woolf?** How the city spoke of nothing that summer but Antoniades, prowling, explosive, shattering, in her black dress on the stairs, her cleavage and glittering earrings. **I am, George. I am.**

Adele thought about this on her way back to the house, the mat of the bay stretched silver behind her, the conversation with Gillespie left in the air down there, by the jetty.

Sonia was still asleep, he'd said, something derisive in his voice. Adele wanted to ask about **where** Sonia was asleep. Did they share a bed, as everybody said? The nature of their relationship was a mystery, though speculation was rife. They were lovers. He was gay. She was gay. But she was married! This was plain fact: Sonia Dreyfus had been married to the constitutional lawyer David Rossiter for forty-three years. Still the rumors persisted: She was married **and** gay **and** the lover of gay Joe Gillespie. He had a mother thing.

They were artistic collaborators. She was his muse. He was hers. She was on the Box Factory board. Rossiter gave the theater millions. Whatever the arrangement was, it had gone on for years.

Gillespie was chewing his lip, and having arrived at her side, propelled by that purposeful stalking across the grass, he seemed to be waiting for something. Adele, nervous, could not go on with the yoga charade. She began moving toward a wooden bench on the boardwalk, as if it were part of her plan anyway, and Gillespie followed. Her arms hurt, and her thighs, and she sank gratefully to the bench. The little dog sniffed around her shoes, which was all right. It was more comfortable here, once they were no longer looking at each other.

The crew at Xander's had had a late night, Joe said morosely. Now that the Chekhov was finishing, they were on to the next thing, working out how to approach the Gorky. He said "we." He meant him and Sonia. He thrust himself forward then, elbows on his knees, staring at the ground. He seemed to be rather angry. Why was he telling her any of this?

Adele said, politely, "Oh." She wanted to leave, because she was filled now with a great boredom. There was the Gorky, before that had been the Chekhov, and after the Gorky would be the Ibsen or the Strindberg. Or the Brecht or the Pinter or the Beckett. Gillespie would do self-deprecating interviews on the internet about the complexity, the insane ambition, of what he was attempting. Audiences would swarm through the doors on opening nights, and in none of it would Adele Antoniades figure for a single moment, and the thought of all of this stupefied her into the same old, dead rage. Except now she was too weary, too bored, for anger.

Gillespie suddenly turned to her and said, "What would you do, if you were me?"

He had asked her a question, and he was looking at her, waiting for her to answer it.

Adele was stunned to see that it was fear in his face. And now she understood he had been **affected** by what she'd said yesterday! Challenged, even hurt a little, by the opinion of Adele. And here he was, asking her for advice.

Something important had happened inside her last night there on the street, she knew now. She had looked at Finn, had seen the indifference and innocence of his body, of his empty mind, and something had fallen away in her. The dog simply sat, and now Adele sat, too, making no sound, taking no action. Waiting. Then all at once she knew that despite the posters and the fuss, the Chekhov had been a flop, that it was the latest in a series of flops, and she knew that Gillespie was sick with terror that some unidentified new boy wonder was climbing the rungs, steadily, furtively, toward his job. And she knew that, in some way, he held Sonia Dreyfus responsible.

Oh, Joseph. She almost laughed. But she could not, for she understood too well the terrible pain of failure. She was his equal, here on the bench. From this point they could begin.

All of this, and the rest of their conversation, Adele carried back with her to the house. It was like a secret, though there was nothing shameful in it. But she could not expose it to the light, especially not to the scrutiny of Jude or Wendy.

She could still play her now. She knew she could, for the broken-glassness of Martha remained inside her, always. Shoulders back, snarling, grieving. It would be original, a new kind of theater. Adele looked only sixty, everybody said.

Behind her came the **slap-slap** of running feet on concrete, and a waft of air as a young woman sidestepped and swept past, lithe and singleted, golden arms and legs. Her ponytail danced beneath the cap, the morning sun lighting up her skin. Well, yes, but what was a girl like that to Adele Antoniades?

She shook her Fitbit, but she couldn't read it without her glasses. She turned up the hill toward the house, slowing a little along the steep path. Wendy and Jude would be awake now, making breakfast. There would be lists of jobs for Adele to do. She didn't want to think about that. Jude giving orders, possibly not making her pavlova after all.

She still had the Martha earrings, they were among her favorite jewels. She had them here, in her suitcase. The wardrobe manager had slipped them into Adele's hand all those years ago, drunk at the cast party. The earrings were heavy and black, they swung and glittered.

Who's afraid? I am, George.

But Adele was not afraid. A new, utterly new kind of light was being born inside her.

When Wendy came back from her walk, Jude was kneeling on the kitchen floor surrounded by saucepans, hunched over as if pressed down there by the weight of her own anger.

Good, Wendy thought, and stepped past her to get to the sink.

"Why are you squinting?" asked Jude, but Wendy was not.

"I'm not," she said, brushing a few grains of sand from her temple.

"Why've you got sand all over your face?"

"I haven't," she said at the sink, and filled a bowl, then a glass, with water. She took a surreptitious swipe at her cheek, but the grains stuck, like glitter.

She went outside and set down the bowl for Finn, who ignored it. She sat at the wooden table on the shady end of the deck. Her body was unharmed. She squinted out from the shade at the bright light and drank cold water from the thick glass in her hand. A little sand in her eye, in the corner, was the cause of the squint. She went to finger it out, but there were specks of sand stuck to her fingers, and now there was a great irritant, a cluster of grains she supposed, moving about her eye.

It would soon be gone; the eye took care of itself. Most of the body was like that:

you left it alone and it sorted itself out. Her body was strong, she'd been pleased to find, pushing herself up from the slippery rock where she fell. She had not even hurt herself, though it was comical, must have been comical for those people to see an old woman go to peer into a rock pool and then oh! Bottom in the air, knees in the sludge, and then whoops! Over again, slipped onto her side. Water splashing everywhere, sunglasses and phone covered in sand slop. Her phone! She recovered and knelt, in the scummy sandy water on the slimy stone, holding her phone. That would be a disaster. She wrapped it in her T-shirt, rolling it up from her waist, tucking it under her chin while she collected the sandy glasses and hat, damp but only a patch wet.

Finn had merely stood, watching helplessly, the lead tangled around Wendy's ankle.

Nobody insulted her by coming to help, which was good, because she was **unscathed.** She felt quite jaunty for the rest of the walk home, once she unrolled the phone and saw that it was okay, only the case a bit damp. Her body was strong, and there was not a scratch on her. Just sand, pressed like glitter into her skin. And this eye, which would look after itself.

"Did you fall over?" Jude was standing in the doorway, spying.

"No," said Wendy, not turning around. Let Jude look, let her try to invade. Wendy was not accountable to Jude. She would endure. She would not turn around, because her eye now had to be fully shut thanks to the sand, and it took all her will not to bend forward to try to empty out the grains. She simply sat, the sandy eye screwed shut and watering, the good one looking out past the silvery boards of the deck, at the trees.

Eventually she heard the clank of saucepans and knew Jude was back at work, so she could sneak past the kitchen door and into the bathroom to wash out her eye. In the mirror she saw that her T-shirt was smeared with yellow mud across the left shoulder. Didn't matter. She splashed her eye and lo! The sand was gone, and she was satisfied and stood, tall, in the small room.

She was troubled by something that had happened on the beach.

There had been a small toadfish washed up, dead on the sand. She was worried Finn would try to eat it, but he was afraid of the waves and did not go near it. Fat little thing, she wanted to stroke its soft white belly. The waves would reclaim it, roll it back. But the tide was going out; a rogue wave had cast the fish too far up the beach, and it lay out of place, on the hard sand. It needed to return to the water, to slowly rot, to desiccate and disperse. Wendy flicked it with the toe of her sandshoe, and there the little slapping wave came, claiming the fish, rolling it over and over, back to the sea, white belly flashing. But then the waves slid back and left it there again, on the sand. It was not to be reclaimed. She and Finn limped on, but it irked, that the waves would not take the fish back. Nature did not always do what was right.

Wendy liked to impose her will, Lance used to say, only sometimes laughing. If Lance were here, she would have told him outright, "I fell over!" And he'd say mildly, "Are you all right?" and she would say of course, and he would agree that Wendy was strong, a small slip and a fall on the beach was nothing, and certainly none of anybody else's business.

Then, though, after the toadfish, there was another thing, down on the sand. It was ghastly. Some sort of creature. An arrangement of what might be fins, or perhaps bones or close-set pointed brown teeth, quite pretty in their arcs, like a clutch of curving tortoiseshell hair combs, tiaras. But then, attached, there was the body. She could look at it for only a moment. Distended, fleshy, slimed, and bruised. Gray and purplish, a long tongue, was it? Or a penis, flattened and rotting? Lying there beneath, attached to, the combs. She clutched the lead, and Finn, too, strained to get away from the thing.

If Lance were there, he'd have been fascinated, turned it over to investigate, but Wendy stepped back, away from it. She and Finn hurried over to the rock pools, and that was where she'd slipped.

She sat on the deck beneath the pepper tree, rubbing her elbow. There was not a scratch on her, and in fact it might have somehow energized her—she practically ran home afterward. People went on and on about falls, as if you went down and never got up again. As if one small slip and that was it, broken hips and nursing homes, begging your daughter to dig up your suicide pills from the backyard. Well, she had fallen and was none the worse. It was a victory. But the memory of the thing lingered slimily in her mind, and she wished she had not seen it.

In a moment she heard Adele pounding up the stairs, then talking to Jude in the kitchen.

She came outside with her own glass of water and sat down. "You all right, Wendy? Jude said you had a fall!"

They had talked about her in the kitchen. This was Adele sent out to placate.

Now that Sylvie was gone, it would be like this. The thought made Wendy want to cry. But she saw that Adele was not thinking about Wendy or Jude but—of course—about herself. "Wend, sorry, but remember I asked you about a little loan?"

Wendy turned to look at her. She'd forgotten all about Adele's asking her for money and that she had agreed. But now her attention was brought to it, she realized again that it was strange.

"How's Liz?" she asked, not kindly. **Why can't she give you money?** she didn't ask, but Adele's eyes when they slowly turned to her were glassy, and she wasn't acting.

"Oh, **Adele.**" Bloody hell. Liz had kicked her out.

"Don't tell Jude," Adele said quickly.

Finn jerked in his sleep and then

shuddered, as if something possessed him for a moment and then flew out of his body.

What Jude was not allowed to say was the plain truth: that Finn should be put down. It was this, not the jobs still to be done or the dog piss on the floor—which was disgusting—that created the bad feeling permeating the house. It was all this lying, all the unspoken things that suffocated Jude at Wendy's every inane remark about him—about Finn, Sylvie and Finn, their wondrous friendship, about the dog being lovely, being fine.

Every time Jude had to hold her tongue, every time she didn't tell Wendy she should pay him the kindness of letting him die, she felt falsehood pulled tighter like a plastic bag, closer, closer over her mouth and nose. She couldn't bear it.

And this bloody house had to be cleared, and Daniel was playing happy families.

He had not yet responded to her last text, which meant he was doing the Christmas bidding of his wife—but what did Jude expect? She was not allowed to be offended, and now the others were sitting around whispering on the deck, so Jude, as always, had to carry on alone.

A moment ago, to offer something, to try to soften the air, she'd gone to the doorway and told them she would cook a chicken for dinner. They'd turned to her with hidden faces. They'd been talking about her.

She didn't care. This wasn't a holiday. Jude was here to work.

Back in the kitchen, she stood at the counter allocating saucepans to camps at either end: keep or throw. The "throw" end was cluttered with the cheap, infuriating nonstick pans with their bowed bases and grazed surfaces—why did people keep buying them, pan after pan, when they always warped in the center and the black stuff was slowly, irrevocably scratched into your food?—and the flimsy stockpots with broken handles, buckled biscuit trays and muffin tins nobody had ever used anyway. "Keep" held three newer stainless-steel saucepans with well-fitting lids and the cast-iron frying pan that only Jude used because other people found it too heavy. And now she made a third—very small—section, of things that she would take home. These were the things she'd given to Sylvie herself.

In the pile were the silver salad servers and her own big red Le Creuset pot in which she'd once taken a coq au vin to Sylvie and Gail's in Sydney and which had never been returned. It was her own fault. After the first couple of times she asked about it, when Sylvie said without guilt, "Oh, yes, we took it to Bittoes, I must remember to bring it back," Jude accepted that the pot might one day reappear or it might not, but that she could not depend on its return soon, or ever. Now the enamel on the inside of the pot was dark brown, blackened in flaky patches with baked-on muck, and the exterior was greasy with fluff and grime.

She sent another text to Daniel—**two more days of this, agh!**—to force herself to be generous toward him, to remind herself that time was passing, that this suffocation would end.

And then she found a bottle of bleach at the back of the cupboard beneath the sink, spread out some newspaper, and got to work on the ruined enamel. She pulled on the rubber gloves and started scrubbing. Sylvie was careless with other people's things, but she was always forgiven, and it was up to you to prevent, retrieve, repair. This was simple fact; all her friends knew it, or should. If you trusted Sylvie with your possessions . . . well, more fool you.

Adele called out from the living room that she would make a start in there and that Wendy was doing her own bedroom now.

Why should Jude respond? Was she their mother? She didn't answer. She scoured the pot Sylvie had burned, holding her breath as the ammonia rose in the air, stinging her eyes.

• • • •

Jude's black mood leaked through the house now, seeping through the flimsy walls and floors. Wendy was glad to hide in the bedroom. Finn clipped up and down again, but the rhythm of his movement no longer made her anxious, now that he was out of Jude's line of vision.

Poor Adele, what would become of her? Wendy filled with exasperated sympathy, and also with a conviction of deep, ruthless self-defense. She could not have Adele at her own house; she needed to work.

Something would turn up, which was what Adele always said. Liz would take her back, or she would attach herself to some new man, or woman. They'd all seen it happen over the years. They marveled at it—the way that, when defeated, Adele could reach inside and strike a match, light the lamp of herself, and turn it up. Then the suitors came, moths to flame.

But Adele was in her seventies now,

came the doubting voice in Wendy's head. Nobody wants you when you're old. You have to shore things up before this point. You have to face the future, the worst possibilities, you have to prepare yourself. Anticipate, adapt, accept.

Wendy began emptying the bookshelf. This room, too, would be easy, for there was really only the bedside drawer—she could empty that straight into a bin without looking, she decided—and the books.

Wendy was not sentimental about books the way other people were. You needed them, they were air for breathing, but as objects they held no sappy emotion for her. And they made her sneeze after a certain point. You could not give them away; she knew that because she had tried. Nobody wanted books anymore; you might as well tear them apart and throw them in the recycling yourself, but instead they were left in boxes on the street until the rain came and waterlogged them or they moved from car to charity shop to dump. And yet each one pulled at you, held a part of you.

But she could be merciless with Sylvie's books, hooking them out of the bookshelf with a finger, one by one. Here was **Watership Down** and **Three Cheers for the Paraclete,** here was **Hoyle's Encyclopedia of Card Games, The Female Eunuch,** and **Seashells of the Australian Coast.** There was a decaying little pile of mystery novels with silverfished covers: **4.50 from Paddington, The Thirty-Nine Steps,** and **One, Two, Buckle My Shoe.** She dropped the lot into the charity shop bag—one, two, one, two. They were Sylvie's books, but even so she could not help revisiting the parts of herself the titles called up . . . the girl reading all day on her parents' bed, the girl flipping shells with her bare toes along the beach, bored rigid on holidays, the time at boarding school, the strange drives with her father to someone's property to stay a few days "to give your mother a break" (from what?)—dusty, unfamiliar houses lived in by shearers or farmhands with whom her father sat drinking beer while she lay on a sagging single bed and read Agatha Christie with her feet paddling the chalky weatherboards of a farmhouse sleep-out.

Wendy sneezed. Finn came tip-tipping to her door and stood staring hopefully, his good eye weeping a little. "It's okay, darling," she said. He stood, and her hand drew out a pile of cards, postcards to Sylvie from people on holidays.

Sentimental old Sylvie! She flipped through them—red London buses, a Greek island, a Hong Kong cityscape—and she recognized none of the handwriting. Scrawled messages from people she'd never heard of, called Daryl, or Cassie and Dave, or Arabella Hoskins. Who were all these people, and where were they now? Dead, she supposed, a good number of them. She tossed the cards, one by one, into the garbage bag. There was one of the Eiffel Tower from Gail—she would keep that for Gail, though it said only **See you on the 14th, bring a coat, it's freezing!** Another, of the Chrysler Building—from her! From Wendy herself! She let a gentle warmth spread through her, that Sylvie had kept it. On the card Wendy had written that she was gobsmacked and inspired and lonely in New York, but the Chrysler Building made it all worth it. She hoped they were all well. **Home soon, Wxxx.**

Wendy remembered nothing from New York except the Chrysler Building and the terrible illness of missing Lance. She sat here in the bedroom, which smelled of mold, trying to remember New York and failing. She felt ashamed, because it seemed to her that the rich detail of the world was precious, but she knew this only after she had missed it. It had been the case all her life: when she recalled things, experiences—walking in Central Park, or punting on the Cherwell with a boy at Oxford, or swimming at the Abrolhos when the baby seal had spun and leaped around her—she realized she had not paid enough attention, and now those things were just outlines, gone. She'd recognized this before, but knowing it did not help. She spent her time storing away the detail while looking forward to the next thing, or worrying about it, knowing that the details would be hers to return to now that she had them accumulated, piled together in her mind's suitcase, but when she opened it, there were only flat, lifeless scraps.

She determined to notice properly now, really concentrate on all experience—the sensation of her ears filling with seawater yesterday, the color of the waitress's eyes—but things rushed toward her and then past, and she could not stop them for long enough to pay them proper heed.

Young people, Australians, now spoke with American accents, pronouncing their **r**'s at the ends of words and saying **afterr,** the **a** like in "apple." Why was this? The Western world had blurred itself into one jellied cultural mass. Her students, last time she'd lectured—years ago, when they still wanted her—knew the names of suburbs in San Francisco or Seattle better than the names of towns of Western Victoria. It was strange. For almost all of Wendy's life, the only thing Australians knew about America were the words "New York" and "L.A." or "Niagara Falls," but now her friends' grandchildren were buying brownstones and running businesses in Brooklyn as if this were the most normal thing in the world. **Neighborhood,** they said. Bed-Stuy. Prospect Heights.

It shamed her that her own world had somehow remained so small despite the years at Oxford, despite New York for those brief dazzling months. It should have been dazzling—**Ms.** and **Esquire** and Columbia, all wanting her work, all wanting the mind, the ideas, the intellectual gifts of Wendy Steegmuller!—but when she looked at this postcard, all she remembered was embarrassment that Americans thought she drank too much and her shock that even some feminists employed black maids. And that she missed Lance so badly, so bodily, it made her sick, and she came home as soon as she could. Oddly, she realized now she had no memory of what they'd done about the children. Who had looked after them? Lance, obviously, but there must have been someone else. His mother? It was a mystery.

There were people who thought she should have stayed longer in the U.S., should have had more courage, that she let down the sisterhood by running home to a man, to motherhood. She'd felt for a little while that Sylvie might be one of these. She rubbed the postcard on her belly to dust it, read it again, and threw it into the bin with the others.

Adele had not quite finished with the top bedroom, but she would do it later. It was dispiriting in there, with the bags of clothes everywhere, the half-emptied cupboards. She would finish it tomorrow, when she had more time. When she had a clearer idea of what would happen next. Who could know? She looked around the living room. Untouched, a stage set, it held all kinds of possibility.

Outside, the cicadas were filling the still

summer air with sound. You must shed the dead skin—this is what she had told Gillespie. The bush was full of insects and snakes reborn, shining with newness. The dried carapaces rustled as the resurrected creatures slithered out of, away from, their dead selves. You had to struggle free from what had protected you.

Where to start? She stood in the room. The teak sideboard, with the sliding doors. You saw things like this in trendy furniture shops now; they were expensive. She wished she'd not thrown out her own furniture from the seventies, but that was like wishing on a star. And anyway, it had been hideous, for a time, before it became beautiful again. Even that ugly globular plastic stuff was fashionable again now.

She closed her eyes, exhaled one long, complete breath, concentrated on softening the muscles of her face, her throat. When you were afraid or uncertain, she had always thought, the trick was to ride it, like a wave. You could not sink beneath it. You went back to basics, and soon enough you could steer yourself, you could control the direction. You could surrender, yet not be beaten. Self-belief was critical. She had always known this, every artist knew it. But last night, that moment with Finn—the stillness of it—had shown her something new, offered her a glimpse into a new realm that could be waiting for her. Resilience had always been one of Adele's greatest strengths, but this was different. This was rebirth.

She'd not said anything to the others yet about tonight; she had not yet found the right moment. She would slip into the kitchen later and just mention it lightly to Jude, when Jude's mood had improved. She would like to ask—but not right now—if Jude still planned to make the pavlova, which she found herself thinking about frequently. It would be a reward.

She opened one of the sideboard's sliding doors and saw the fraying cardboard lids of board games and jigsaws. That would be very boring. She closed the door, slid open the cavern of the next section:

records! Sylvie had always had a terrific record collection, still keeping her turntable here when everyone else got rid of theirs. Adele took hold of a wad and pulled it out, and as soon as she saw the covers—Linda Ronstadt, Pink Floyd, the Rolling Stones—whole phases, intense experiences, of her life came flooding in. The early years at the Old Tote, the Ensemble, the Channel Nine years, all that **work**! New knowledge moved through her—it was like a blood transfusion—that creation was still there to possess, that within her reach there remained not only the same possibility but something else. Something better.

People thought that when you got old, you wanted your lost youth, or lost love, or men, or sex. But really you wanted work and you wanted money.

Jude found Adele sitting on the floor, dusky record covers fanned out around her on the carpet. The room was in chaos.

Cupboards and shelves had spilled their contents everywhere—no corner of the room was clear—and the garbage bags lay folded, untouched, on the dining table.

"I'm sorting them," said Adele simply, without looking around. "They could be valuable." Then she held one before her, her face lit with joy. "Look!"

The Mamas and the Papas, dressed in pullovers and trousers and cowboy boots, were all four lying crammed in a bathtub. A toilet sat alongside them. The image made no sense at all.

Adele slipped the record from its cover and—Jude was quietly irritated at how she could simply raise herself from the floor like that—skipped across the room to put it on the turntable, fiddling with the buttons to see if the player still worked. There was a clunk, and then a blast of "Monday, Monday" came furrily from the enormous black speakers.

Mama Cass had choked on a ham sandwich, was the joke. Jude held the record cover, looking at how the other, thin woman's body was draped over the bodies of all the other band members, along the length of the bath. All you could see of Mama Cass was her head. Everybody loved Mama Cass, but nobody wanted to look at her. A flicker of Jude's old food revulsion came alive in her gut. It was a long time since she'd been sick like that, but it stayed there inside her, part of her muscle and skin and bone. Mama Cass did not choke on a ham sandwich; she was found dead from a heart attack, poor woman. She had died alone.

Adele hummed along with the music, cross-legged on the floor once more, lazily sorting records into piles. Jude noticed then that looped against the walls and over the curtain rail were strings of ratty silver tinsel and fairy lights.

"Adele!" she shouted above the music. "What have you been doing?"

Adele looked over her shoulder, following Jude's gaze. "I found them in a drawer.

Don't you remember? Sylvie put them up every year!"

She saw Jude's face. "I know you've canceled it, Jude, but for some of us it's still Christmas."

There was a noise on the deck—Finn making a low, pained moaning. Jude could not help returning to the kitchen window. The dog had his muzzle thrust through the railings, distressed by something in the bush below.

Before thinking, she found herself on the deck to see what was bothering him. Below them a brush turkey stepped, hauling the strange black swag of its body along, stepping and halting, kicking detritus aside, its oddly small head jerking as it moved. Finn's gaze was fixed on the bird. The shrunken balloon of its lurid yellow wattle swung at its throat. He grew more agitated every time the bird moved, jerking his own head, pushing his snout farther, more painfully, between the bars of the railings. Jude called to him, but he could not hear her, and then she was beside him, comforting, thumping his smelly coat. "Come on, old thing, don't worry. It's only a bird."

She pulled the dog gently out from between the railings, talking softly. "Come on, settle down, it's all right now." He turned his face toward her, but she could not meet his animal eyes. Something was happening to Jude that she didn't understand. Her own eyes filled with mystifying tears, and she moved back into the house, into the kitchen, to work. Through the living room door, she saw Adele, kneeling impossibly on her haunches like a teenager, her shoulders moving in time with the music as she sang along.

For some people it was still Christmas, Adele had said, but what did that mean? It surprised Jude that she had not considered the question, ever, in her life. Daniel's wife would be wrapping presents for him to give to the grandchildren. Daniel would be halfway through nine holes of golf now, and on the way home he would stop at the Wine Cellar to load crates of alcohol for the next day into the back of his Saab.

Christmas was supposed to mean renewal. It meant the beginning of things, not the end. But Sylvie was dead. Really dead and not coming back, no matter how much you wished she weren't dead, no matter how much you wanted to see her, hear from her.

Jude felt a fierce, physical longing for Daniel to be here, now. She wanted the tall strength of his body beside her at the pantry door. She wanted to put her head against his chest and surrender. To what? She didn't know. But he wasn't coming just yet. She took a breath, returned to her work, careful not to look out the window where she knew Finn was facing her, seeking her, staring up through the glass.

Wendy wrestled another bag off the inclinator, down the last few steps to the row of bags already slumped alongside the boxes of junk on the verge. They had thrown out so much already, but inside the house things looked untouched. It was endless, and boring. She wanted to be finished, to have a holiday. To think about her work to come, not decaying paperbacks and clothes and cockroach-eaten bits of paper. She shoved at her bag, which was filled with books nobody would want, she was sure of that. On the top, peeping through the tied handles, was **The Tibetan Book of Living and Dying.** Very old-hat now.

Birds squawked in the trees above, and cars made their way along the roads. Other people were out and about, preparing, greeting one another, readying for Christmas, which was the end of the year and also a beginning, bringing new things into their lives. She felt claustrophobic, stuck here with Jude and Adele. She needed to get on with it all. Those two lived in the past too much. They had regrets and longings for things gone. Even if Jude didn't talk about it, you could see it in her, the losses, the things she hadn't done.

Sylvie, like Wendy, had been free of all that.

Well, she was really free now, Wendy thought sadly. She looked down at **The Tibetan Book of Living and Dying.** Had Sylvie actually read it? Everyone had a copy, back when they used to like talking about death, when they were young. Or youngish. Wendy would make a bet that Sylvie hadn't read it at all, even back then. She herself had read only a few pages, but she remembered Jude especially going on about it. How you had to get yourself ready, you had to embrace it, she'd said. Back then Jude talked about her image of death: a white, curved place of stillness and a kind of holy silence. She made it sound like the damned Guggenheim.

Wendy looked around the street at the houses, the trees. At the world: the rich, tawdry, unjust, destroyed, and beautiful world.

None of them talked out loud about

death anymore, not even Jude. Although plenty of others did; it was a hobby for some people, they loved it. Janet Schofield had even invited her to some sort of **club** to talk about it. No thanks. And a friend of Claire's called herself an "end-of-life doula." "What's that?" Wendy had said. "Palliative care without the qualifications?" But this Katie had smiled serenely at Claire before answering Wendy that **doula** was a Greek word meaning "woman of service." **Bugger service,** Wendy wanted to say. **Haven't you ever heard of feminism?** She didn't say that, of course. She said, "Ah, well, good for you," and tucked the pamphlet into her bag, and when she got home, she threw it in the bin.

The cicadas had begun their glorious, maddening shriek. Wendy looked along the street and felt gladdened by it all, by the motley gardens and the cars and the houses. Old and new, everything mixed in together. Little saplings springing up, peeling clapboard cottages alongside the ridiculous modern concrete-and-glass jobs.

This was life, this was what should happen. The big mess of it all, together. She pulled the strings of the garbage bag tight and tied them again, and **The Tibetan Book of Living and Dying** disappeared beneath the plastic.

At four o'clock Adele bent before the open fridge and asked for the fourth time today about the damned pavlova, and now she wanted to know whether there were any prunes. She held a packet of prosciutto in one hand.

"What do you want prunes for?" snapped Jude. Why was Adele asking such things? It was Jude who shopped and planned for and made all the meals when they were together, Jude who made sure that the meals were pleasing, made sure the others had not to lift a finger in the kitchen except for the washing-up. This was one of the observations she'd sent to Daniel, in a lengthy text to which he had not yet replied and which made her feel sheepish now. Daniel declined to fan the flames of these sorts of remarks and would chide her about it later, gently, in person. **But, Judo, you** like **being in charge of the cooking.**

Once more she marveled at the world Adele occupied, watching her crouched there at the fridge. It was as if its interior were a new land she was discovering—she drew things out, read their labels in surprise, put them back. A block of halloumi, a tub of yogurt. Ordinarily Adele took no interest in food until it appeared on the table, when she sat eagerly, joyfully helping herself. Plunging in, delighting in it. She did the same with all material things—clothes, bedrooms, sofas, wine, swimming pools, throw rugs, chocolate—assuming that anything in her field of vision was available to her, was put there for her ease and pleasure. As if life were a hotel suite paid for by someone else and the someone else was naturally overjoyed to have Adele there to vivify it all. Sylvie had been a bit like that, too, taking things that were not hers to take, assuming you wouldn't mind.

Liz obviously didn't mind anyway. Which was lucky.

Adele had changed her top and had freshly pinned her hair into its extravagant pile. She looked lovely. She was exasperating. The living room floor, Jude knew, would still be scattered with record covers and all the drawers pulled out of the sideboard. Adele had done nothing the whole day but sit around hooting at album covers, shouting out non sequiturs about things they brought to mind—the red front door at the house she'd shared with Jack Thompson once or which play she'd been performing when Carly Simon's **No Secrets** was released.

There were prunes, in fact, though Jude had pushed them to the back of the fridge. She did not discuss her body's private rhythms and discrepancies with anyone. Such conversations between women made her blanch, with their expectation that she, too, would share the details of her own bodily functions and malfunctions. But she never did. When they were young, she'd refused to discuss her sex life the way her friends did. They laughed at her, called her Jude the Prude until they found out about Daniel, which confused them.

Her contemporaries still spoke about their bodies with self-absorbed fascination. Her neighbor in the apartments, Barbara, had once cheerfully confided in the car park that a sneeze while she was hanging out the laundry had obliged her to pop back upstairs to change her knickers, and she cackled softly in an all-girls-together sort of way. Jude had felt her face stiffen in disgust. Another time Barb had confessed relief because finally, after several days, she'd "gone." Jude avoided her as much as she could. But Barb was by no means alone. Adele and Sylvie used to have long, luxurious conversations about hair loss or diarrhea or "dryness" (Jude didn't ask). They would lift their blouses to show each other some mole—called, obscenely, a "senile wart"—that had arrived or, more surprisingly, fallen off. If Jude happened upon them talking this way, they found her distaste hilarious. **It's just bodies, Jude,** they'd sing. Once, when she could not stop herself from a sigh of revulsion and turned back into the kitchen, she heard Sylvie diagnose her with a murmur: fear of death. And Sylvie and Adele had laughed out loud at her retreating back.

"I was just remembering devils on horseback," Adele said now, into the fridge.

Jude snorted. Devils on horseback. It must be the old records.

"I'm making two salads, and we have the chicken," she said flatly. For heaven's sake.

Yes, but this would be for before dinner, Adele told her. Just in case.

"In case what?"

"Well, people might drop in for a drink or something," said Adele, looking deliberately into the fridge rather than meet Jude's eye. "It's Christmas Eve."

What was she talking about?

Now Wendy called out from the living room, "This is very nice; who did all that?"

Jude stepped through to see Wendy, fists on her hips, looking around at the spotless room. The records were piled in a small, neat stack on the sideboard, the table wiped clean of dust, and in its center a silver candelabra was set with three tall red candles. The piles of papers had vanished. Jude could not see where everything had gone, but she was certain Adele had not actually sorted it all. It must be shoved into a cupboard somewhere. The mirror at the far end had even been polished. The curtains were drawn open, and the windows shone. Beyond the deck the bay gleamed like pewter. The fairy lights Adele had strung along the curtain rods and picture rails made the room glow with sweetness.

Jude stood, stunned, and then there was a jolt and a rumble: the inclinator jerking into life. The women looked at one another and went outside.

On the deck they stood, peering down to see Sonia Dreyfus and Joe Gillespie arranged on the little platform, creeping up the hill toward them. Sonia, borne aloft in her carriage, gazed out at the dominion of the bay. In her arms she held a small white terrier, convulsing, barking its head off.

CHAPTER NINE

■■■■

"Coco! That's enough!" chided Gillespie.

The white terrier skittered from room to room, sniffing and letting out its sharp little bark. Adele had ushered Gillespie and Sonia into the house, welcoming them magnanimously, as if this were her own place, but now she glanced anxiously at the dog, then Jude, and said to them, "Let's sit on the deck. We don't want to waste the view!"

Sonia was already out there with her back to them, gripping the railings, staring down over the bay. She wore black, a sort of jumpsuit with a deep V neckline, and gold and silver bangles rattled along her slender forearms. The pants were long and loose, and her gold sandal heels—fine and narrow, the sort that could easily get stuck between the veranda boards—peeped from beneath the hems.

Gillespie lurched around the living room after the dog, but Coco did not wish to be caught. Jude turned just in time to see the dog eyeing the wide white expanse of the couch, preparing to leap. "Not on the sofa, Coco," she said loudly, nudging the animal firmly with the side of her foot, so the little dog stumbled sideways. Gillespie looked at Jude, shocked.

At the admonishing sound of Jude's voice, Sonia turned and cast a cold gaze over her, looking first at her T-shirt, then appraising her shoes, her pants, her jewelry, landing at last on her face. Jude saw with satisfaction that Sonia was not accustomed to having her long, critical stare returned in kind. She was surprised at the jab of loyalty she felt to Adele, who was now fussing in the kitchen, rinsing champagne glasses in the sink.

Wendy reappeared. She had vanished down the hall, muttering, "Dear God in heaven," when she saw the visitors approaching. Now she was back, her hair brushed and wearing a bright coral lipstick that made her look mad. She had put on a clean white cotton blouse and a pair of floral-printed trousers. Both were crumpled; the trousers had horizontal fold creases across the thighs. Jude felt another pang and at the same time wished she'd had time to change her own clothes. But she would not alter herself for the likes of Sonia Dreyfus.

Sonia looked older in real life—of course the photographs and posters erased all lines and sun spots, leaving only the strong jaw, the wide-set eyes—but still there was something magnificent, threatening, about her. The slow turn of the head, the stance, the sweeps of eyeliner. Jude's mother's ancient bitter talk of enemies and rivals rose inside her. The word "whore" shimmered, faded.

Adele called in a bright voice, "Here we are!" and came carrying a wobbling tray of champagne glasses, stepping too carefully over the threshold in her silly pink sandals. Jude noticed now how low cut was Adele's T-shirt, how tight her trousers—they must be Liz's, the way the fabric strained across the bum. The famous boobs were offered up, décolletage trembling a little now as she struggled with the tray. The glasses tinkled as she lowered it to the table; Jude reached out a hand to help her, but Adele's sharp glance stopped her.

Wendy stood watching. "Oh, wait!" she said. "I have something!" The deck boards shook under the tread of her big flat feet as she made toward the kitchen. Sonia watched Wendy go and then looked around for Gillespie, still indoors at the sideboard shuffling through Sylvie's records, Coco sniffing around his feet. Who,

Jude wanted to know, had invited him to touch anything?

"Coco!" Sonia barked, as one would call a child approaching undesirable playmates in the park, and the dog trotted to her side. Then she called, "Joseph!" in exactly the same voice. But Gillespie remained at the sideboard, peering at the text on a record cover in his hands. It seemed to Jude that he was deliberately ignoring Sonia, who stared. She was not used to being disobeyed.

Adele pushed at her hair with both hands and then began picking at the golden foil wrapping on the bottle. "It's French," she said modestly. There was a nervous shine to her voice. Jude had seen this nasty stuff in the fridge. It was French, but not good; it was the cheap, supermarket, large-bubbled sort. She could already taste its sour taint. They all watched Adele struggling to find the point at which to rip off the foil; her nail varnish had bled into the tiny cracks in her cuticles, and Jude noticed for the first time how speckled were her hands. She saw Sonia looking, too, saw that Sonia's own nails were perfectly trimmed and clean, bare of polish. Jude wanted to take hold of Adele's hands, hide them. She wanted to wrench the bottle from her and hurl it over the balcony. Why had she asked these people here? Didn't she see how they despised her?

Jude looked around for Finn, was glad she couldn't see him. She hoped he was asleep somewhere. She realized she did not want him exposed to the cold stare of Sonia Dreyfus.

Wendy hunted for her chiller bag in the kitchen, but it had vanished in Jude's purge. She'd left Finn sleeping outside her bedroom, and he had mercifully stayed there—she must keep him away from the little dog, who would frighten him.

She opened the pantry to see Jude's grocery collection that stood in place of Sylvie's bottles and cans. Everything Jude touched looked curated, designed, like a gallery display—but off to the side, quarantined, was the assortment of Wendy's packets and jars. "Adele, wait, I have something!" she shouted, pulling out a squat jar. There was a squeal from the deck as Adele's cork popped, and the wine overflowed as she poured it into glasses. Wendy rushed from the kitchen with her jar—it contained a ruby red, jammy syrup with deep crimson blobs in it—and wrenched off the lid. "These are marvelous," Wendy said, spooning a glob into each glass before Adele could stop her.

"What **is** that?" Adele asked uneasily, hovering. Wendy showed the jar: Wild Hibiscus Flowers in Syrup. "It makes champagne into a cocktail!" she said gaily. She had never tasted it before. She'd found it in her pantry and thrown it in with the other stuff.

Sonia and Gillespie each held a glass carefully, by the stem.

"Merry Christmas!" toasted Adele, and they raised their glasses. Wendy saw the dark jellyfish of the flower looming malignantly, sliding toward her mouth as she drank. It looked like a blood clot.

There was a moment of reverent silence, and then Sonia spoke. "Absolutely delicious," she said in a voice that meant **absolutely foul,** and put her glass down on the table.

The terrier began barking in a high, insistent staccato, and they turned to see that Finn had limped around the corner of the veranda. He stood, appalled, his shaggy, noble head held back as the little dog danced and shouted around him.

"It's all right, Finny," soothed Wendy. Beside the young dog, Finn looked even worse than usual. Moth-eaten, crippled and dirty, more bewildered than ever. Sonia and Gillespie both stared at him. You could imagine them saying horrible things in private.

"How **old** is it?" asked Gillespie, staring in repulsed fascination.

Wendy moved to Finn's side, positioning

herself between him and the little yapper. **Mind your own beeswax,** she wanted to say. "He's seventeen. And he doesn't cope very well with a lot of people. Or other dogs," she called over the high barking. But nobody moved, so Wendy pushed at Coco's pointy little face with her hand. "Shush," she said. "Off you go."

Coco yelped, and Sonia called, "Come here, sweetheart, Mummy's here." She scooped the dog into her arms.

Gillespie had not stopped staring at Finn. "Jesus Christ."

Two long, dirty threads of drool had formed, drooping and swinging from Finn's open, panting mouth. Wendy was shot through with guilt. "He only does that when he's very **stressed,**" she said, a barb of malice sharpening in her now. Why were these people here with their nasty little animal, torturing poor Finn who had never hurt a fly? He shuffled slowly backward, then turned a few times and went to stand with his face tucked into the far corner of the deck, where the railing joined the house. His trembling had begun once more. He stared, diligently, at nothing.

Gillespie watched, amused. He went over to Finn and inspected him closely, then grinned at Wendy. "What's he actually looking at?"

"Nothing," snapped Wendy. She was about to say, **Get away from him,** when Adele patted the veranda rail beyond the table and said, a polish in her voice, "Ooh, look at the big cloud bank coming, Joseph. You don't get this view anywhere else on the bay."

Wendy and Jude, who met her eye, were not the only ones who noted Adele's "Joseph." Sonia Dreyfus was on her feet in an instant, thrusting herself into the space Adele had made.

Jude rose from the table, saying pointedly that it was time for her to get dinner started. Gillespie and Dreyfus appeared not to hear her. Wendy, afraid, followed her, and stood with folded arms in the kitchen doorway, keeping an eye on Finn, who remained at the end of the deck and continued his staring.

They hid in the kitchen for an hour. “What on earth is she doing?” whispered Wendy, standing in the doorway. She looked from Adele to Sonia and back again, then watched Jude working, dabbing at the flaccid chicken carcass with a paper towel, then pushing her fingers between the flesh and the skin, separating, tearing. The raw bird jerked on the board under the force of Jude’s fingers. She just shook her head grimly in answer to Wendy’s question. She stalked from counter to fridge to sink to counter.

Daniel had not replied to any of her messages since this morning. She reasoned with herself: this was normal, she had sent only three, there was nothing urgent for him to respond to. It was Christmas Eve, family time, what was he supposed to do?

He would be here in two days. Still, offense fizzled up.

She forced a lump of herbed butter beneath the cold white-pink skin of the dead bird, kneading and squashing, holding the opening closed, stretching and smoothing the lump down, forcing it farther into the crevice between thigh and breast. At some point tonight, or tomorrow, Daniel would find a quiet moment and ring her, and they would laugh about his brother's dolt of a son. She would hear how well he'd done with his gifts, what kind of glaze he'd made for this year's ham. And how Helena thought the day had gone.

At times she'd felt quite sisterly toward Helena. Obviously, she knew; it was not possible that almost forty years of this could go by without her knowing. And yet, Daniel swore, she had never mentioned it. Never challenged him, never questioned his frequent short absences. She was a sensible woman; Jude admired her restraint. She knew it was unlikely Helena admired her in return. Only the smallest part of

Jude thought this was unfair. Small but, it surprised her to notice, increasingly potent. It seemed to be surfacing more often these days—a little spurt of dismay at knowing she was probably hated, despite asking for nothing, expecting nothing, from Daniel. Despite at all times respecting his family's prior claim. Surely there was something to be admired, over forty years, in that?

She flipped the chicken over, dabbed at its slippery back.

Certainly Daniel's Nicole hated her guts. She knew this, had known for at least twenty years, because Nicole had told her so: twice in letters, once to her face at an unfortunate accidental meeting at a party. It was many years ago, but it still caused Jude pain—a little pain—to know this. She would like to take Nicole out for dinner and explain what a very small part Jude played in her father's life. How little their relationship needed to affect—how little it did affect!—Helena, Nicole herself, any of them. But this could never happen. The time Nicole approached her at the party, her eyes bright, her countenance so shockingly like Daniel's that tears began to come to Jude's eyes until she forced them away, Jude beamed a generous—a genuinely warm, that was important—smile at Nicole, spoke in her calmest, lowest voice, and told Nicole that she was sorry, she had to go. She made it clear her apology was not about Daniel but about their meeting like this. She made sure not to embarrass Nicole in any way, but nor would she submit to Nicole's idea of her; she would not be shamed. Then she moved smoothly away, her restaurant training serving her perfectly, allowing her to move easily through a room, touching an arm, murmuring a greeting, becoming gradually invisible while all the time she felt that her heartbeat might shatter her breastbone. And she had slipped out of the house moments later and gone home, poured a very stiff glass of scotch, and slept badly.

• • • •

The smell of roasting chicken floated out to the deck. Wendy went out again to check on Finn and to refill her and Jude's glasses—minus the hibiscus flowers, which Jude had tossed into the sink and then the garbage. Sonia's untouched drink remained on the table with its awful betraying clot; she refused another, clean glass.

Sonia and Gillespie were having a long and complicated argument about "the Gorky." Sonia issued her sonorous opinions; calm, authoritative. But something was awry. Gillespie slouched in his chair, prising a gray splinter of wood from the table edge, not looking at Sonia while she spoke. Adele tottered around the deck, filling Gillespie's glass and her own, passing the dip for Sonia to gouge into with her cracker, offering her own little interjections. Vassa, surely, said Adele, was a symbol of doomed capitalism. Sonia paused a moment to allow Adele's voice—an unavoidable distraction, like a passing but distant airplane—and then continued as if Adele had not spoken. **Don't you see, Joseph.** Patient, teacherly, but Wendy heard the plaintive note in her voice. And there was a lower, sharper edge—of fury, that she had been brought here to compete.

Gillespie looked from one woman to the other, sullenly picking at the table. A teenage boy resenting, resisting, two possessive mothers. Adele held the bowl of dip and tossed her hair. She wore weirdly enormous, swinging black earrings.

The whole scene was pitiful. The desperation of the women, the young man's cold, expectant judgment.

The knowledge came to Wendy then that it was true, that something had happened to her Jamie, not only the time in the hospital but before, and afterward. Her son had suffered. She did not know how, and she had been unable to prevent it—but only now did she fully understand that he held her, his mother, accountable. That's what Wendy couldn't get out of her head, watching this young man, watching his contempt for Sonia Dreyfus intensifying by the minute. Something had not gone right for Joe Gillespie, and now here he was, blaming, punishing. Wendy felt ill watching Sonia's incomprehension, her silent, growing panic.

Jamie had been wounded in some way, but she wanted, madly, to cry out to her son, **It was not my fault! Life itself causes us pain, don't you see? And you are** young. **See here,** she wanted to say, **look at the natural supremacy of the young.** See Gillespie, who, sitting here in Sylvie's house, does nothing but wait, receive. Here on the stage set of a wooden deck high in the trees, all the attention, all the neurotic need of two—three—fully grown women was converging on this vain, cosseted boy.

The cloud bank was deep and dark now, moving quickly.

Thunder sounded unevenly across the bay; fat raindrops began smattering down. Wendy bustled about the deck, swept up Finn's bed and the towels, grabbed him by his collar, and pulled him into the kitchen. "There's a storm starting," she said to Jude, defiant, daring her to complain as she pushed together Finn's bed and towels, making a nest for him on the kitchen floor.

He squatted, quaked. Jude looked at him, then at Wendy, and said, "He'd just better not make any **mess.**"

Sound came bursting in—it was Adele and Gillespie laughing, gasping, as they dashed from the rain into the living room. Silent Sonia Dreyfus settled herself in the center of the white sofa, Coco at her feet.

"This storm looks as if it will be quite severe," Jude called into the living room. "Not good for driving."

But they appeared to be going nowhere. Gillespie resumed his earlier meander about the room, picking up Sylvie's things and examining them with acquisitive interest.

"Check this out!" he said to Sonia, lifting a heavy blue glass bowl shaped like a curling wave.

Until now these things had simply been Sylvie's things, unremarkable, familiar as their own old possessions: the bowl, the green vase, the amber glass water jug with the frosted gold bands and its matching set of little tumblers. Now, under Gillespie's scrutiny—and, more menacing, Sonia's—the things became objects of amusement, of assessment. "You've got one like this, right?" said Gillespie to Sonia, putting the bowl down with a thump. "I guess they were the thing, back in the day." He moved along the sideboard.

Jude, who must have seen this through the doorway from the kitchen counter, called loudly, "Wendy, would you set the table, please? It's getting late, the chicken's rested."

Adele jerked around, sending Jude a betrayed look. But she turned back to the others and said sweetly to Sonia and Gillespie, "You'll stay for dinner, won't you? There's plenty of food."

The rain was louder now; the glass doors juddered at a gust of wind.

Sonia smiled from the couch and said, "Oh, **God,** no, the others are expecting us."

"But Jude has made her amazing chicken! You can't miss that." Adele was desperate.

Sonia said, triumphant, "I'm afraid so. But thank you for the lovely drink."

Get out, Wendy pleaded silently. **Go.**

Adele's face fell; she was beaten. Her ridiculous earrings dragged in the slits of her earlobes. She looked tired now and—Wendy saw with tender sorrow—quite fat.

"Come on, Joseph," said Sonia. She leaned down to scoop a skinny forearm through the loops of her handbag. You could see the bones of her thin chest.

Gillespie had not turned around, was still holding the cover of Neil Young's **Harvest** in both hands. And then something changed in his body. "Actually," he said lightly over his shoulder, running a thumb and forefinger along the cover's frayed opening to find and pluck at the tantalizing edge of the record's slippery cellophane sleeve, "I might catch you later." He drew out the record, flipping it expertly.

Wendy thought again of Sonia and

Gillespie entwined, dried branches on a bed.

Sonia's smile hung as she screwed her bangles higher up her wrist, sitting there on the couch, waiting. Her skin twisted with the bangles, ruching the flesh of her forearm. Coco had snuffled across the room to Gillespie's feet and stood looking up at him. Now Sonia could not keep a faintly urgent note from her voice.

"Joseph, we need to leave these ladies to their Christmas holiday."

It's not a holiday, none of them said. Gillespie turned to face Sonia, his hip nudging a little closer to Adele's there against the sideboard.

"The rain is heavy now," Wendy said. "Might be best to get away before the storm really hits."

But Gillespie met Sonia's gaze. "I'll stay, I think." He turned to bestow on Adele a dazzling, seductive grin. Then he turned back to Sonia. "I'll help you down to the car, though. In a minute."

Sonia seemed to have been pressed back, ever so slightly, into the cushions of the couch. Gillespie bent to lower the needle to the record. He would not come across the room to help her from the sofa; she was left to wriggle and awkwardly launch herself upright.

A slow, hollow drumbeat came from the speakers: once, twice, and then a third, flatter, meaner beat.

Sonia turned to Jude and Wendy as if noticing them for the first time. "Thank you so much, this has been **lovely,**" she said in her deep, hypnotic voice. The drumbeat: one-two-**chshh,** repeating. The women stared at Sonia Dreyfus, because it was as if she were now illuminated from inside. Wendy felt it, and Jude surely did, too—the stark, golden beam of her attention. She kissed them each on both cheeks. It was something, this beam. Unsettling, charged, supremely powerful.

A whining harmonica phrase twisted out of the speakers along with the beat, and Sonia's illumination dimmed as she turned her gaze to Adele, calling coldly, "Merry Christmas, Adele." **I despise you.**

"Coco!" she summoned, but the dog sat by Gillespie's feet. She called again, more harshly, and the dog puttered to her side. Gillespie made to cross the room to say good-bye, but Sonia would not be pitied. She stopped him with a look, then snatched up the dog. "I don't need you," she murmured, and turned out of the door to the deck.

An enormous black umbrella flowered above her, and she stepped onto the inclinator platform, slamming the little gate closed behind her. Jude and Wendy stood under the narrow awning, watching her descent. She was still magnificent in the darkening evening, her silver jewelry glinting, Coco glowing white in the gloom, as the rain clattered down.

When she was gone, they turned back and saw Adele through the window, leaning in to Gillespie, giddy with ambition and victory, and the insect boy leering back at her over the records.

"What are you doing, you foolish girl?" whispered Jude.

At the table Joe was still talking, but Adele watched Finn through the kitchen doorway. He lay on his bed on the linoleum, staring at a point beneath the stove, innocent and dreaming, at once present and somewhere, something, else. It flickered again, the thing she had felt in him in the street. He yawned now, and his head slowly, slowly lowered, then snapped back, alert. He just was. **Here I am.** Adele breathed it in, felt the air change around her. Something immense was happening to her.

Joe went on and on; she heard his youth and ambition and torment, but she heard the music, too, and she was elsewhere now, on her way, reaching the place. She had dreamed it once. Dreamed of a lifting, rising sensation in her body, and first she was afraid but then surrendered to it as her feet left the pavement and she floated up, up, to another, invisible plane of existence, and there she found the real people, her tribe, all living and working, another whole realm, a gracious, flourishing society, and they welcomed her in.

And how surprising that here it was, her moment; the ailing dog was teaching her, showing her. The music's drumbeat changed, and Finn sat bolt upright, and she saw there must be no delay, no fear now, between impulse and action. Everything she had done before—even Martha—was wrong, and now a lightness whipped through her because she **knew** what to do, how to move and speak as Martha, completely transformed. Her animal self, not her conscious mind, would lead her. She was all creaturely receptivity, looking around the table and seeing them as if for the first time: Joe Gillespie, Jude and Wendy and their need, their sorrow and fear. A new, astounding compassion for all things—for her friends, for the past, for Liz, even for poor Sonia—flowed through her.

At the table they sat, a horrible foursome, passing dishes back and forth. Wendy could not bear the way Adele kept putting food on Gillespie's plate, kept leaping from her chair to change the music and bring more wine. Gillespie droned on about the petty minds of the Box Factory administrators, about the doddering subscribers, everyone's lack of artistic vision. Adele kept nodding, though to Wendy it seemed she wasn't actually listening. She refilled Gillespie's glass and her own, while Jude and Wendy put their palms down over theirs. She laughed in a strange, dreamy way, tilting at the windmill that was Joe Gillespie.

He helped himself to three servings of the chicken, the crusted vegetables. He ate greedily. "**Fuck,** this is good," he said with his mouth full. He used to be a vegan, he told them, but not anymore. He waited for their approval. Wendy and Jude ignored him, chewing silently. Adele said in an absent, wistful voice that she believed in openness to all things, all transformations.

She seemed not exactly drunk but in some elevated state, some trance. She used an unnecessarily wide movement of her arm to pull back her hair, allowing Gillespie a good view of the freckled crests of her breasts.

Dusty Springfield was belting it out on the record player. Gillespie peered attentively down at Adele's cleavage. In acting, for instance, Adele went on. A good actress, a real actress, had an infinite range, could never be restricted to this or that role or age. Her voice grew louder, more grating, as she pridefully listed the leads she'd played, counting them off on her fingers—Lady Macbeth, Masha, Mother Courage, Blanche DuBois, on and on she went.

Gillespie, Wendy saw, was not listening

to a word Adele said; his thoughtful staring at her breasts was incidental. He was very drunk; he might as well have been looking at a pudding.

And on Adele went, now listing roles she would still love to play. Lear, Brutus. Why not? If Glenda Jackson could do it, Harriet Walter, and what about a transformation of some previous, some rediscovered—not looking back but forward, a kind of **reincarnation,** indeed. . . .

Dear God. Wendy gaped; at the same moment she saw Jude's recognition, too. This was what it had all been about: the flirting, the preposterous earrings. Adele had some ludicrous fantasy of clawing back her one great moment on the stage, from thirty years ago. It was grotesque.

Jude rose and began aggressively clearing dishes. Gillespie was slumped in some floating reverie of self-love and grievance, elbows on the chair arms as Jude collected his plate—like a waitress, like a handmaid—and swept from the room. Adele sloshed more wine into Gillespie's glass, sang loudly along with Dusty that someone should tear out another little piece of her heart, to cover the sound of Jude crashing the dishes into the kitchen sink.

Gillespie looked then at Adele's face and grinned. "You were right, y'know. Back in the park." He was slurring. "I need to start again. Get rid of all this shit." He waved his arm to encompass a whole circle, gesturing at something beyond, behind them all: the town, the theater people, Sonia?

Adele was soaking up the radiance of his praise, but Wendy knew it wasn't praise. She felt a dangerous, vengeful urge. She felt a great violence pulsing inside her, pushing her to lean across the table and slash at Gillespie's arrogant young face with a blade.

In a moment she was by Jude's side, scraping the remains of the cooking pans into the bin. She'd flung a few pieces of chicken into Finn's bowl. He lifted his head from the bowl and watched her, then sniffed again at the meat.

Jude was whisking cream now, elbow

whirring. "She wants to go back and play **Martha**!" she hissed.

Wendy took four dessert bowls down from a shelf.

"Liz's kicked her out," she said flatly, and Jude stopped whisking.

In the other room, the music grew louder as Adele turned up the sound, and the rain beat even more heavily on the tin roof, and Finn stopped nosing at his food. He began shivering and turning in circles on the kitchen floor.

Joe flung open the door to the weather as the rain thundered down. It was thrilling, stepping out to join him on the deck in the noise, the streaming air. Adele sweated, prickly with revelation as she held out her hand for the big doobie he was sucking on. He grinned at her in a surprised, wasted way as he held in his breath, then passed the joint to her.

His fingertips met hers, and she looked

down toward the bay, but it had vanished in the dark and wildness. Familiar things had disappeared, borders, boundaries. It was clear to Adele that Joe knew she would help him, that he needed, even desired her. This was no longer a surprise: she simply had to be, to allow. She felt her earrings swing as she tilted her face under the awning, and she exhaled the long, slow, delicious breath of smoke. **I am, George.** She smiled as she passed the joint back and he reached for it again. He knew, and she knew, and the plume of smoke was a long feather of possibility stretching out for Adele Antoniades now, the dark of the stage beckoning to her. Standing on her mark, all the muscles of her body taut with potential, her vocal cords satiny, eyes shining with wit and Martha hurt and her spirit willing, willing, willing.

Behind them in the room, Manfred Mann burst from the speakers.

"Oh!" She nodded at Gillespie, for it was time, and she pulled him by the hand into the house. The lights were low, and she danced across the room to the volume knob and turned it way up, and she and Joe met in the music and the past and the present, in the sway of their bodies and everything new that was opening for them now.

What Jude and Wendy saw, carrying in the pavlova at this moment, took on the quality of a painting, of a dream. They saw Adele and the man step into the light from outside, saw Adele transformed, holding his wrist and moving around him, tempting and laughing, raising her arms, answering the music.

Jude and Wendy had always understood that there were moments in which Adele existed more fully, with more intensity and truth, than other people experienced over a lifetime, and this was such a moment. You couldn't take your eyes off her, the way she moved in the soft, low light, the music ballooning to draw you all in. You tasted sugar and wine on your lips, and Adele's shining face in the dark room became a point of eternal stillness and grace.

They all saw it, this fleeting, austere greatness.

The ghost creature Finn felt it, too, looking on. He stood in the doorway, watching. Did he fear it? He knew it, the great gathering, the loosening of all things.

Adele and Gillespie threw back their heads and sang, and then Jude and Wendy saw that they were mistaken. They saw that Gillespie was not dancing with Adele but laughing at her, at crazy Adele Antoniades dancing with her eyes closed, hands in the air, a pissed old luvvie spilling out of her clothes, and they saw that he had already pulled his phone from his skinny hip pocket and raised it on this awful vision of failing Adele and he had pressed Record.

At this moment the sky's tremendous light split the room and the thunder struck, and the space all around them was torn open by a low, tortured moan from Finn as his thick old body exploded into the room.

The power was out. The record player was silent, had blown its fuse. The air was filled instead with the awful noise of Finn moaning and scuffling, burrowing into the space beneath the coffee table. Jude towered, shaking with rage, and cast Gillespie out. Adele, bewildered, stumbling and plucking at him, wailing, "Don't go." But Gillespie chortled as he pushed his phone back into his pocket and said, "You old girls are fucking hilarious," and he turned out of the house into the lashing wind and rain. Adele scrambled after him.

In the candlelight the pavlova sank into itself on its plate.

Wendy was at the coffee table, trying to drag Finn out. He had rammed himself beneath it and was cowering, turning dangerously, as if he might shit.

Adele came in through the open door, sodden. "He's gone!" she cried.

"Stop shouting, Adele," Jude said quietly, and began once more collecting dishes. "Close the door."

"What have you **done**?" shouted Adele.

Wendy called to the dog, "Come on, Finny boy, it's all right."

Jude said, "He was filming you, Adele. He thinks you're a joke."

Adele sank into a dining chair, undone. "But I'm going to **help** him!" she cried in disbelief—how could they not see? Yet she could feel it draining out of her now, her beautiful discovery, dissolving and vanishing. They had destroyed it. She began to cry.

The lights flickered, came on again.

Jude did not speak, only shook her head and went on gathering, controlling. Jude the martyr, Jude the boss, crashing dishes.

Finn, cowering beneath the coffee table, moaned.

"Be quiet!" bellowed Wendy at the others, on her knees now trying to get at him, cramming herself into the space between the couch and the table. She clutched at Finn, so terrified now that he **snarled**—at her, at Wendy! But at last, with all her strength, she grasped his coat and hauled the poor frightened creature out, and they fell onto the sofa, Finn scuffling over the couch, the cushions, as he scrambled to be free. She held him, hugged him hard.

Jude, marching in from the kitchen, saw them on her sofa, and roared, "Wendy!"

"Oh, shut up, Jude!" Wendy yelled. "It's a couch, for Christ's sake," clamping Finn's writhing, petrified body to her own. She'd had enough.

"It isn't your house, it's Sylvie's!" she cried. "**Sylvie** loved him. Finn came from Sylvie, don't you remember?" She rocked him, held his shuddering body.

"Came from guilt, you mean," said Adele. She threw it down.

Wendy looked at her and saw her face, which was frightened now, but it was too late, and Wendy said, "What?"

The walls cracked, the trees smacked themselves against the house. She held Finn.

"Shut up, Adele," warned Jude. Adele must not, but Wendy knew it was coming, tried to cover her eyes and her ears, but it was too late, she could see it coming out of

Adele's mouth, the thing from the beach, out it slithered in a disgusting mass about Lance: Lance and Sylvie.

Jude was trying to drag Adele away, but she was a pane of glass, gloriously shattering.

Lance and Sylvie, when Wendy was off in New York being her famous self.

Wendy couldn't breathe. The Chrysler Building and Sylvie and Lance. Finn moaned and finally leaped, freeing himself from her grip. He stood on the couch and gave one mighty convulsion and then began vomiting up a pale mound, a mess of chicken carcass and brown liquid. He stared at Wendy with his dark, horrified eyes as he shuddered and lurched. Wendy stared at the vomit, stared at poor Finn's jolting, exhausted body.

Adele, terrified by what she had done, was desperate now. Trying to take it back. It didn't happen. It didn't matter. "I'm so sorry, Wend, it was only twice," she pleaded. "It was only twice, so, so long ago."

Wendy cried and cried, hands over her

face to protect herself from this ugly, long-known, dreadful truth.

The air was all electricity. They were suspended, Wendy pinned on the couch, Jude and Adele each separate, adrift. None could reach the other. The door was still open, and the rain swept in; darkness had swallowed the room.

The trees flung themselves, writhing, and in one almighty crack the storm broke open the last kernel of the night, and into this Finn let out one last sound, there was a scrabbling, and he was through the door and gone. Wendy went after him, into the wild black night.

The vomited chicken lay on the couch, its murk seeping into the silk.

Neither of them shouted Wendy's name. They knew she wouldn't return. Her ghostly form disappeared down the stairs, calling and desperately calling for Finn in her thin, high, old woman's voice.

CHAPTER TEN

The rain pelted sideways as Wendy scrambled down the wet wooden stairs, clutching the railing, calling out to Finn. She could hear his heavy panicked movement, half running, half falling, ahead of her on the stairs. The wind wrenched at the black shapes of the trees, and her wrists were slapped and whipped by the shrubs as she gripped the railing, pleading for him to stop.

She could no longer hear his slipping claws, his terrified whine.

She reached the bottom and ran into the street, already breathless, her thin clothes drenched. Some streetlight bulbs had blown, but she could make out slender black branches, torn from trees and hurled to the ground. Shreds of bark hung from telephone wires.

She shouted for Finn, but she knew he could not hear her, and her voice disappeared into the wind. She searched the dark for his shaggy white form, listening for any sound of him, but there was only the wind and the rain, the shifting thumps and cracks of thunder. He surely could not get far ahead of her, with his arthritis. But he'd fled so violently, with shocking speed, propelled by terror. She called and called.

If Finn were younger, if she were, this dread would not be filling her now. The few times he'd fled in past storms, he had always found his way back to her. But now his instincts were failing him, he could no longer save himself. He was old and damaged and incapable, and he needed her protection. Of all that had just happened, this was the worst: she had not protected him.

She pleaded into the night. "Fin! Finny Fin, come on, boyo, it's all right!"

But it was not all right. Sylvie and Lance, and as soon as Adele's words were in the air, Wendy had known they were true.

Her feet slipped awkwardly, the hard leather of her thongs rasping between her toes, and her left knee sent out a twist of pain with every step. **Come back, Finn.** Her clothes stuck to her body. She had to keep wiping water from her eyes as it streamed down from her forehead. She looked around her in the street. Colored lights still blinked here and there, but mostly the windows were dark.

If he made it as far as the bay, it would not be all right. It was a long time since he'd understood what water was, could do. He no longer recognized edges, or danger. He might not remember how to swim.

She shouted louder, her voice growing

hoarse. As she walked, a part of her lifted out and away, and she saw what anyone watching the street from inside their dry houses would see: a sodden old woman, barely dressed, wandering, crying out in the rain and the dark. Her pale gray hair streaming down her back. Alzheimer's, they would think. Where was her family, poor demented thing?

Who was her family now?

The black road glittered, and there was a deep, blank moment where every surface around her vanished, and then that darkness was ripped open into day with a detonation deeper and louder than anything Wendy had ever heard. She found herself on her knees in the lumpy grass by the low rock wall near the jetty.

Then came Finn's terrified noise.

She scrambled to the edge. He was down there, she could hear him. Huddled beneath the jetty boards on the tiny crescent of sand, up against the rock wall. It was low tide. She shouted, finding her voice again now, and scraped herself tumbling down off the wall, crawled beneath the jetty boards to him. She tried to drag him out but had not the strength, so she crawled in to him, turned herself to lie with him against the wall, curling on the cold sand. She wrapped herself around him, trying to warm him with her body, trying to save him with her old, damaged, incapable love.

The storm began to ease, moving out to sea. The roaring wind had faded, and the rain slowed to a light, steady fall.

She shivered on the wet sand. Slowly she crawled out, then hauled Finn by the collar, using all her strength, from beneath the jetty's boards. She wished she had brought the leash, but once she got him onto the grass above the rock wall and sat there, it became clear it would not be needed; he would not leave her side, pushing in so close beside her she almost lost her balance. She kept hold of him, stroking him, speaking in a low, calm voice, and she could feel his fear slowly subsiding. If she could get him moving, get a calming rhythm into him. She climbed heavily to her feet, and so did Finn. They stood in the dark and the soft patter of the slowing rain.

They could not go back to the house. She had absolutely no idea what to do. She couldn't even get into her car; the keys were in her room. The truth had opened inside her, black, sticky, and catastrophic. Jude and Adele and Wendy: no more. It was all smashed.

Oh, Lance. Oh, Sylvie.

She began to cry again, silently now, as they walked over the grass, Finn waddling beside her, the arthritic dip of his gait returned now, but worse. Her own knee still hurt like hell, and her hip, but something in the movement was helping. Her thongs still rubbed on her raw, wet feet, but Finn was calmed by the familiar pacing, so she couldn't stop now. They reached the road again, and on the smooth asphalt Finn plodded along beside her, his head nodding in time with the matching dips and tilts of their painful steps.

She stopped for a moment to wring out the ends of her flapping pants, did the same with her T-shirt. Things slid through her mind, appearing and receding, looming and falling away. Images and impressions from the past: Lance and missing him, his body, her grief. Jamie in the hospital, the things that had been kept from Wendy, things she'd refused to see. She thought of how powerfully Lance had loved her. She'd believed it. And Sylvie. Strangers, both.

The moon appeared now and then between sweeping clouds, and in those moments of cold light, Wendy saw this: **my life has not been what I believed it to be.** The black tar shone on the road, and here there were cars parked end to end along it, rooftops curved and gleaming. Somehow, in all this wreckage, someone was having a party.

As they rounded the bend, she saw a

small weatherboard hall, faint light glowing from its windows. She was exhausted. She needed to stop, to rest. They came to the hall; she climbed the wooden steps, and Finn climbed, too, his body slow and sore.

It was not a hall but a church. It was midnight Mass.

They stood in the little peaked alcove at the entrance, looking in. Water dripped from Finn's coat, from her hair, to the floor. The power in the church was still out, but around the altar were a number of enormous candles. A couple of dozen people stood facing the front, and low blue lights came from the phones they held in their hands. Here and there someone held a ridged white plastic cup sheltering a candle, the kind used by carol singers. A young priest—Filipino, Wendy thought—stood in a white-and-gold robe, arms outstretched. In the quiet room dotted with the low moving lights, in his golden king's brocade, he was a figure from childhood, from myth. His sneaker toes were visible peeping from beneath the hem of his gown.

In a moment the people sat, and Wendy felt her body could no longer hold her up, and then the priest saw her. He called out, “Hello, come in!” in a matter-of-fact way, and gestured for her to enter—yes, all right, the dog, too. Faces turned to see the deranged, sodden wretch of her. They changed expression; some hardened, some were curious. Halfway down the rows of pews, Wendy saw a family shifting, a woman beckoning. They had made room, and Wendy did not care what they were seeing, for she was so tired, and she and Finn moved gingerly along the green carpet runner of the aisle. She nodded her thanks to the woman and her children, their father. The children stared as Wendy let herself sink down onto the wooden bench beside them. Finn, in the aisle, stepped in his slow, agonized circles—one, two, three—and then sank his haunches down on the carpet and in a moment was deeply asleep. The priest began to speak once more in his soft voice, and the wet-dog smell of Finn rose to join the incense and the candle smoke and the pine scent of a Christmas tree.

Jude and Adele drove the streets in silence, curving and turning to sweep the car's high beams into parks, along jetties. At last they saw light flickering in the windows of the little church, and Jude stopped the car.

Before she turned off the headlights, they saw that the storm had destroyed a nativity scene arranged on hay bales beside the church. Mary's blue plaster gown was visible beneath a bent sheet of corrugated iron; shepherds lay about on the ground.

Communion was taking place when Jude stepped inside and scanned the pews. In the middle of the aisle, she saw that the line of people were sidestepping around Finn, and her body flooded with relief. He lay slumped on the carpet, his belly swelling and subsiding with each breath. Wendy was beside him in the pew, her wet hair trailing down her back, head dropped to her folded arms. Nobody comforted her as they all stepped around her to join the line.

Jude slipped into a seat at the back of the church. A clunky piano rendition of "Silent Night" was playing on a tinny sound system somewhere; the worshippers sang along in their shy, high voices. They were aging and young, holiday families and locals, the men in linen trousers and patterned shirts, or cargo shorts and Velcro-and-nylon sandals, women in bright cotton dresses and blouses, shiny silver earrings. Raincoats and umbrellas were stuffed beneath the pews.

The people eased their way out of the pews and joined the line, stepping forward to the priest to hold out their cupped hands, trusting in this ancient, nonsensical, holy thing, accepting bread from a stranger. Taking it into their bodies. She watched the tilted faces, the opened mouths and waiting hands, and she thought of being fed, being a baby. From somewhere deep in memory came the sweetened nicotine scent of her father's fingers. The people, fed, turned away with their hands clasped, chewing softly. They filed past the chipped plaster stations of the cross dotted along the walls, returning to their seats. High above them all hung a stylized wooden Jesus on his cross: brutalized, naked, sacrificed.

Jude found herself kneeling on the narrow pinewood plank, where others had knelt year after year, betrayed or afraid or suffering, unforgiven or relieved. She felt her bones heavy inside her flesh. She looked at the crucifix. All that savagery, and there was no God, and nobody had been saved, and still they talked about rebirth, beginnings.

She looked at Finn, willing Sylvie to show her face again because Jude was ready, at last, to see her. But when Finn woke and lifted his head and turned to see her, Jude, he was just an animal. A creature, ailing.

The Communion line ended, and the priest went about his tidying at the altar, wiping brass chalices with a white cloth, putting little bowls and glass jugs on a tray. The music started again, a fuzzy piano introduction to "Hark! The Herald Angels Sing." Jude knelt there, resting her head on her crossed hands, the long-gone hymns of childhood returning to her. There was no God, and she was in this world alone, but she sang the words anyway. **Peace on earth and mercy mild, God and sinners reconciled.**

Adele waited in the car in the dripping silence. She felt sharp and bleak and entirely sober. She had said no to entering the church with Jude. She knew that Wendy would be inside, and there would be talk of sin and saviors and redemption. Out here under the bits of corrugated iron by the sodden hay bales would be a plaster baby Jesus and his dead parents, there would be broken animals—a donkey, sheep, camels. There would be a painted backdrop, a yellow star, a destroyed angel.

Adele had done an unforgivable thing, and it could not be repaired. Jude had offered her no comfort as they searched the streets, but nor any blame. She said, "It was always going to come out. It always does."

Afterward Wendy and Finn walked alone in the dark, away from the happy chat and murmur of the churchgoers. Jude and Adele caught up and stepped alongside them. The rain had stopped.

"Wendy," said Adele softly.

Wendy could not answer, because there was nothing to say. She was swollen with sadness. The street glistened, rinsed with darkness and quiet. There was no wind now. The three women made their way along the road, and there was Jude's car waiting. Adele opened the back door and held it there for Wendy and nodded at Finn. “Let him in,” she said.

Wendy did as she was told. Adele closed the door after her and got into the front passenger seat. Wendy sat in the back, Finn pressed to the floor at her feet. She stroked him quietly, over and over, and Jude eased the car out onto the road. The radio was on; Christmas choral music floated softly into the space of the car.

Adele twisted around in her seat. “I’m sorry, Wendy,” she said quietly. “I am so sorry. I didn’t mean to ever say it.”

Wendy rested her head against the glass and looked up to see patches of the stars through the drifts of dark cloud. Brilliant, distant. All that fire and violence, so far away it was only specks. Cold, glittering dust.

As the car moved through the narrow streets the headlights lit the silent green lawns, the low fences, the corner shop. A ragged loop of red tinsel hung, dripping, from a veranda rail. Unmoored, Wendy thought. At either side of the road, the asphalt surface was a broad lake of rainwater and the road now a long, thin island along which they must travel.

The choral music ended, and in the silence Jude's phone chimed loudly. The car moved smoothly along the black road, and the white shapes of the boats glowed on the quiet water. A radio announcer read through Christmas stories. Santa Claus had appeared at a reindeer park in Sweden; meetings were taking place between Muslims and Christians in Bethlehem; emergency services were already cleaning up following a savage storm. Jude pulled into the driveway of the house, and she looked at her phone. The car had stopped and come to a rest, and then Jude made a dreadful sound.

The headlights cast two arcs of light on the pale stone of the wall before them. Jude read, stricken, holding her phone in one hand while the other moved to clasp the top of her head. She had not yet turned off the ignition. Adele took the phone and silently read the message, from Daniel's number: **my father will not regain consciousness. do not come near my family. nicole schwartz.**

Adele passed the phone to Wendy. The women sat in the airless car, suspended in catastrophe. Jude, who had never needed them for anything, turned and looked from one face to the other. She searched Wendy's face, then Adele's, then Wendy's again. Her tongue came out to dab her lower lip. There was the sound of all their breathing.

"I don't know what this means." She said it in disbelief, to the windshield. Then she stared at them again. "What should I do?" Her voice was faint. She had always known what to do: Wait for Daniel. Talk to Daniel.

It was Adele who took hold of the moment. She searched her own phone, swiping and scrolling. It was on Twitter. Philanthropist and former Westpac chairman Daniel Schwartz had collapsed at a family party, suffered a suspected stroke. Royal North Shore intensive care.

"Give me the keys," said Adele. "Wait

here." She got out, dashed up the stairs into the dark.

Cool, salty air came in the open door. Torrents of fear and sorrow sluiced through Wendy. "Jude," she said. Finn sat, awake now. She put her hand to Jude's thin stiff shoulder. Jude might flinch or scream, but she didn't move. She didn't turn around.

Adele was back now, at the driver's side of the car. "I'm driving. I'm fine."

She helped Jude out, bundled a pile of dry clothes and towels through the door at Wendy, and then took Jude around to the passenger side and guided her in.

"Seat belts." Her voice was full of calm authority as she buckled herself into the driver's seat, put the car into reverse, and swept smoothly out of the driveway.

Wendy shoved and pushed at Finn, maneuvering, spreading a towel as best she could beneath him. He made a long, high noise for one piercing moment, then fell back to sleep.

• • • •

For one and a half hours, they drove the charcoal highway, its white lines appearing and disappearing beneath them, the bushland whipping past. Adele was a good driver: confident, assured. Nobody asked what would happen when they got to the city.

What happened was what was always going to happen for Jude.

What happened was that at 2:35 in the morning they parked the car in the street, woke Finn, and tied him—still half asleep—to a pole. They guided Jude, stiff with terror, into a brightly lit hospital foyer, then into the small space of the lift, then along a wide corridor and into the intensive-care waiting room to find a nurse at a desk behind glass. She was sympathetic, and sorrowful, and she turned them away.

His family was with him. Immediate family only, she was so very sorry.

At 3:48 they still sat, in the peppermint green vinyl chairs in the empty room. Jude stared at the dark geometric carpet. And then Daniel's wife, Helena, and his daughter, Nicole, and his son, Ben, emerged from a pair of wide white doors.

Ben looked so like his father that Jude's inhalation was audible.

Without looking in the women's direction, Daniel's family walked with their arms linked past the waiting room, out into the corridor, the elevator, down to the foyer, and out through the sliding doors into the dark street.

Still Jude could not be admitted. They returned to the desk, one by one. Adele coaxed and charmed. Wendy was officious, entreating. Jude, finally, begged. She was turned away.

There in the waiting room, she cried, aloud and completely, her face pressed into her thin, elegant fingers, her long body cradled and rocked in the arms of her friends.

• • • •

It was dawn when they drove back into Bittoes. Adele was still at the wheel, alert, steering them down the winding hill. She turned left, to the beach. It was no longer raining, but in the distance over the ocean was a bank of dark cloud, another storm happening far away. The sea was deep green in front of them, the light pale in the sky as they pulled in to the car park.

"Come on," Adele said.

Wendy picked through the pile of towels and things Adele had snatched from the hall and thrown in the car last night and found their swimsuits. Jude, speechless, did as she was told.

They climbed out of the car into the humid air of Christmas Day. There was nobody about as they moved gingerly, stepping from their clothes, pulling on their swimsuits. Adele pulled a fallen strap of Wendy's suit up over her left shoulder.

They walked in single file along the

furrowed sandy corridor to the open beach. Finn limped along behind them. When they neared the water and Adele dropped their towels on the sand, he did not flinch, showed no agitation. He slowly walked around the three women, stopped, and circled them again. And then he flopped down on the sand and curled his great shaggy tail, resting his face on his forepaws.

Adele looked at Finn, and he saw her. Here they were.

"Come on," she said again, and led her friends to the water's edge.

The ocean was fresh and cold against their flesh, and each woman gasped with the creep of the water up her thighs, her belly. The sea was cloudy; long, dark rags of weed were pushed about in the water.

Adele ducked under the surface, and then, coming up from beneath a small wave, she looked behind her to see Jude's face: shocked, alive. Afraid. Wendy, too, was fearful as she watched the swell growing in the distance.

Adele floated on her back, her gaze to the sky. Then she swam to the others, to where their feet could all touch the bottom, the water at breast height. She reached out, Jude taking one hand and Wendy the other, and she felt their hands grip hers as they stood on tiptoes, the current lifting them now and then from the sand.

Wendy looked across the deep green field of the ocean.

She knew that soon the vet must come and let Finn die in quiet ease on her couch.

Lance had slept with Sylvie. Sylvie had been with Lance. It was true, and this meant that other things were untrue—that Wendy had ever known Lance. That she knew Sylvie, or herself. This would stay with her forever. She did not know that in a number of years' time, swimming at another beach—after she had sat in a room in Prague with Jamie and his husband, after Claire had helped her pack up her house, after her book was published, acclaimed—some stark facts would clarify themselves to her. These facts would separate from the weeds in the cloudy water: That Lance had not always been unhappy. That he and Sylvie had acted not from cruelty but from loneliness. That she, Wendy, had made a great many mistakes, and yet the simplest thing remained: she had loved Lance, and Lance had loved her. It would be the plainest, strongest knowledge ever to take root in her.

But all that was far away from now. Watching the wide green sea on Christmas morning, she had to understand her life, her children's lives, from the beginning again. From here.

The water gripped Jude hard around her chest, tight and cold. She looked to the horizon. Between the sky and the water was a thin, thin line. That was where Daniel was, and where she must now live, with a trace of him behind her eyes, in the cartilage between the bones of her chest. She would go back to her apartment sometime, perhaps tomorrow—it was probably no longer her apartment—and wait.

Adele felt the salt water tightening her

skin. Sylvie was dead, Liz didn't want her, the future was unknown. She had lost, she felt, a great deal. But here in the water, her frightened friends were gripping her hands. Holding on to Adele for dear life. The swell grew, larger and larger. Jude and Wendy feared its approach, feared the great unrolling wall of water, but Adele kept firm hold of their hands and called, "Don't worry. Go under when I tell you." She made them wait, the strong instrument of her body persuading, and she counted and said, **"Now."**

And each of the three let go, plunged down and felt herself carried, lifted in the great sweep of the water's force, and then—astonishingly gently—set down on her feet again. They breathed and wiped their eyes, reached for one another again, waited for the next wave.

ACKNOWLEDGMENTS

This book has had many benefactors. Foremost among these is Judy Harris, patron of the Writer in Residence Fellowship at the University of Sydney's Charles Perkins Centre, a multidisciplinary research center committed to improving global health. This is a visionary fellowship bringing art and science together, and I was honored to be its first recipient. My sincere gratitude to Judy and the center's academic director, Professor Stephen Simpson, for their faith in me and in the program. Thanks to the many researchers who welcomed me and offered help, especially Professor David Le Couteur, Professor David Raubenheimer, Dr. Lise Mellor, and Joel Smith.

Some of this book was written at the Stella Grasstrees Writing Retreat, and I am grateful to Carol and Alan Schwartz, the Trawalla Foundation, and the Stella Prize for this beautiful and generous gift.

Thank you to my agent, Jenny Darling, publisher, Jane Palfreyman, and editor, Ali Lavau, for their sensitive and expert guidance over many years, and to Christa Munns, Louise Cornegé, Christine Farmer, Jane Finemore, Matt Hoy, and all at Allen & Unwin for their care.

For helpful conversation and other acts of generosity, thanks to Elizabeth Alexander, Tegan Bennett Daylight, Lindy Davies, Sandy Gore, Naomi Hart, Vicki Hastrich, Lucinda Holdforth, Heather Mitchell, Eileen Naseby, Jane Palfreyman, Ailsa Piper, Prue Sargent, Carolyn Swindell, and Linden Wilkinson.

Always and most of all, thanks to Sean McElvogue.

ABOUT THE AUTHOR

CHARLOTTE WOOD is the author of six novels and two books of nonfiction. Her novel **The Natural Way of Things** won the 2016 Stella Prize, the 2016 Indie Book of the Year, and the 2016 Novel of the Year in her native Australia, and was joint winner of the Australian Prime Minister's Literary Award for Fiction. In 2019 she was made a Member of the Order of Australia (AM) for significant services to literature.